DIRTY TALKER

A Slayers Hockey Novel

MIRA LYN KELLY

Melissa, Hugs from the Slayers Hockey hunks!
Mira Lyn Kelly

Copyright © 2021 by Mira Lyn Kelly

All rights reserved.

No part of this book may be reproduced in any form or by any electronic or mechanical means, including information storage and retrieval systems, without written permission from the author, except for the use of brief quotations in a book review.

DIRTY TALKER

Photographer: J. Ashley Converse Photography

Model: Austin Loes

Cover Designer: Najla Qamber, Najla Qamber Designs

Editor: Jennifer Miller

For Kara Hildebrand

Chapter 1

Wade
Off-Season

Another fucking club. Not my scene, but Boomer and Bowie love this shit, Axel too. They can't get enough of the velvet rope and VIP treatment. The noise that passes for music, and the lights that require a photosensitive warning.

They thought they'd be safe hiding out here, but enough is enough.

I cut past the muscle with a rock the size of my thumb in his ear to the balcony end of the room where my teammates are sprawled across a couple weird-shaped couches surrounding something that's supposed to pass for a table.

Boomer's the first one to see me and yeah, that

guilty look and elbow jab at Bowie say I was right. They were hiding. *Pussies.*

Axel's back is to me, but when he turns, it's with the lazy smile that says he couldn't give a shit that I found them. Typical. "Hey, man. Sign your new contract yet?"

"Not yet." And I'm not about to be derailed by talk about my NHL contract when I've got bigger fish to fry. Dropping into an open club chair, I eye each of them in turn. "Swear you don't have an available sister, cousin, or trusted friend you're holding back on me."

I'm supposed to be home in less than a week, and if I show up to my brother's wedding without a date—

Shit, I can't take another week of apologizing and coming up with polite ways to extract myself from one soul-baring conversation after another. From the hope and heartbreak and pained disappointment that make me feel like the world's biggest asshole.

Boomer starts picking at the label on his beer and Bowie's suddenly mesmerized by the ceiling. Meanwhile, Axel, that fucker, looks me dead in the eye and shrugs.

Christ, I'm the guy who can talk anyone into anything. Yet somehow, not one of these dicks is willing to cough up a sister for me. "What the hell, man? I'm a good guy."

Nothing.

"*I'm dying here.*"

"Uh-huh."

I huff, because that's how far this has gone. I'm arguably one of the toughest sons of bitches—after Static anyway—on the Chicago Slayers hockey team. And I'm *huffy* because my friends won't share. "That's all you've got to say?"

"What do you want me to say, man?" Axel rakes a hand through an overlong hank of hair he won't cut again until preseason. "I've got all three… plus a single brother two miles down the road. But you can't have any of them." He meets my eyes again, no fucking nonsense in his. "I don't pimp my sister out for weddings. My cousin would straight-up stab me if I so much as suggested she let one of my teammates act like she was his. And I keep my friends by not asking them for bullshit favors, especially *week-long ones*."

More like ten days, but that clarification sure as hell isn't going to help me out.

Axe sits back. "As for my brother, he's a dog. He'd be banging the bride before the rehearsal dinner was over. You can do better."

I'm weirdly touched, but that still leaves me screwed.

I turn to Boomer. "Come on, man. I know you've got a sister. Just let me borrow her. One week. Please?"

Ben Boenboom's one of those guys with a resting

goof face. He's friendly, always grinning at something. But not now.

"*Borrow* my sister?"

Uh-oh.

"A week? Of sharing your *bedroom*?" Bowie leans in next to him, his scowl taking on a menacing glint that reminds me these two have been friends long enough he's probably as protective of said sister as his roommate.

Boomer's eyes go hard. "You can fuck right off."

"Dude, I'm not trying to bang your sister. I would *never*—"

"Try to borrow my little sister for a week of sleepovers?"

Ten days. But, Jesus. "Yeah. That."

The guys sit back with matching nods that has me pinching the bridge of my nose.

All I need is one girl. Something I've never had any trouble getting. There are women aplenty in the crowded club, bunnies lined up at the bar, just waiting for the signal to come over.

Water, water everywhere, and not a drop to drink.

I can't bring any of these girls home. If anything, it would make the whole situation worse.

But now that I'm thinking about it— "What's with the bunnies?"

Usually, they'd be doubled up on Boomer's lap

by now.

"Axe won't let us invite them over," he announces sullenly.

I raise a brow, turning to Axel. "No?"

"Got a friend stopping by. A *friend*. You know, the kind of woman I don't dip my wick in, and therefore can ask to be my date for a wedding without worrying about her getting the wrong idea. Also, she's married, so don't bother trying to poach her."

"Ha-ha-ha." *Dick*.

"There she is." Axe whistles, holding up a hand to where a dozen girls are making their way up the private staircase. It's a tide of short dresses, stacked heels, and giddy laughter rolling in.

I should get out of here. Let these guys have fun while I go home and—

Whoa. No way.

From the sea of feminine faces, one stands out from the rest.

I know her. *Sort of.*

Harlow Richards works at the bank. Not on my accounts. But I've seen her on the private banking floor. Ridden the elevator with her. Noticed she wasn't wearing a ring and might have tried chatting her up a time or two.

Tried being the operative word there.

It's her. I recognize those burnt-umber eyes and the

way she twists the soft spill of her hair over her shoulder. That lush mouth when she takes a sip of whatever girly drink is in her stemmed glass.

I wonder what kinds of plans she's got over the next few weeks.

Ha, forget that.

The only thing I know about this girl is her name, and that's because I talked it out of the coffee cart dude from the lobby. I might need a date, but no way am I bringing some unknown quantity home for more than a week with my family. Not without a solid stamp of "psycho-free" from a reliable source anyway.

Still, she's got my attention.

It's curiosity more than anything else. With the way my hockey career is finally coming together, I don't have the bandwidth for a relationship. But a night or maybe just a couple hours?

Who knows.

Harlow's not smiling. Not scoping out the exclusive area of the club like she can't soak it in fast enough. Not devouring me and my buddies—because, despite the fact that they won't share their sisters, that's what they are—with starstruck, or even curious, eyes.

Maybe this isn't her scene either.

But she's veering off from the party, walking our way.

Walking toward *Axel*, who's standing up to greet her.

Only he said his friend was *married* and… Then I realize she's not alone. And it's *her friend* who's sort of happy-dancing into Axe's open arms with all the thanks for setting her up with the VIP access for her friend's party.

My teammates invite the girls to join us, and I settle back into my chair. I might be screwed as far as a date for my brother's wedding, but maybe this night has some potential yet.

Harlow

JOCKS. Like this night wasn't bad enough already.

Taking a greedy swallow of my Snowflake Martini, I slide into the open spot next to my work wife and wannabe life coach, Annette Quinto, offering an absent wave to the guys parked around the table as they introduce themselves. Under any other circumstance, I'd at least feign polite interest, but tonight—and possibly for the first time in my life—I just don't have it in me.

Whatever. Pretty sure these athletes' egos can handle it.

Turning my phone over in my hand, I glare at the department-wide email congratulating Junior on the job that until sometime in the last twenty-four hours had been mine.

"Turn that thing *off*," Nettie chides, grabbing my hand in hers and muscling the phone back to sleep. "Forget about the promotion. I know it sucks. I know it's not fair. But give yourself the night off from thinking about it."

Right. A night off *was* the plan.

I don't take them. Ever.

Finishing off my second Snowflake, I don't feel any better. I haven't loosened up the way Nettie swore I would. And worse yet, *I still care*.

And I *hate* that.

Almost as much as Junior's smug wink when he'd walked past me on the way to his new office.

When will I learn?

Nettie's talking a mile a minute to the guys surrounding us, becoming best friends with them the way she does with everyone else. The way I don't do with anyone.

The blond one with the goofy smile asks about the party, wanting to know who the bride-to-be is and which girls are single.

"Yeah." The grumpy-looking one beside him waves to the guy in the chair. "Grady here's after a date for his brother's wedding next week."

"I'll go!" Nettie squeals, and I can't help but laugh. She's a grab-life-by-the-horns kind of creature, and it's one of my very favorite things about her.

She would not be sitting idly by while someone with less than half her experience took the job she'd been working toward for the better part of a decade. She'd be letting headhunters woo her and entertaining offers for positions that were better than the last.

She wouldn't be taking two weeks off while the "restructuring" shook out and a new position was found for her.

Why is my drink empty?

Nettie's friend, or rather client—both?—shakes his head with a chuckle. "Sorry, babe. It's for the *whole* week. And he needs someone willing to pretend to be his *girlfriend*."

My brows inch up.

The one who needs a date groans. *"Dude."*

Ouch. Well, at least I'm not the only one facing down embarrassment tonight.

Client Dude waves him off. "Relax, Nettie and Harlow handle our money. They're not running to TMZ."

He's right about TMZ. We would *never*. But the money? Not quite. While Nettie's a senior account manager in the sports division of private banking, I don't work with anyone's money directly. In fact, until the announcement this afternoon, I'd been heading up compliance.

Nettie taps a red-tipped nail against her chin, giving

Dateless the once-over. "But you're hot."

It's true. His body is insane, if you're into that solid-packed-muscle thing.

"Why can't you get a date?" She turns to Client Dude. "Is he a dick?"

Dateless tips his head back and covers his eyes with the heels of his hands. And whether he's a dick or not, the bulging thing that happens with his biceps and already broad chest is kind of *wow*.

"Nah. Grady could probably land a date before our next round arrives." And like he was some kind of magician, a girl in a short, glittering dress breezes in and starts unloading drinks… including another Snowflake Martini for me. Client Dude winks. "He just can't score the *unicorn* he's hoping for."

Goofy shakes his head. "Fucking picky. He wants a girl who's not into him in any way. A girl who won't get ideas."

Wow. What a catch.

But then this date-thirsty, built egomaniac shakes his head, shooting what looks like a worried glance… my way? "Yeah, because I don't have time for a girlfriend right now, and I don't want to end up hurting someone's feelings."

Dateless, don't worry about me. I don't handle your money and I don't care.

Only, I guess I do. Because there are a lot of jerks

out there who never factor in other people's feelings.

Nettie nods slowly. "I thought all you pros had teams of people on staff to help you out with stuff like this. Isn't there some pop princess your PR team can pair you up with?"

Goofy answers for him. "Sure, but what happens when her IG feed blows up the next week with some boy-bander's tongue down her throat? Too easy to debunk."

Grumpy adds, "And said unicorn needs to come with references. No more than two degrees of separation."

"Right, right," Nettie agrees, a furrow digging in between her brows. "You don't know whether she'll sell your story to the *Enquirer* or take a kidney while you're sleeping."

Okay, and I love Nettie. Because the expression on poor Dateless's face right now? He's totally thinking of his kidneys. And it's pretty funny, actually.

I have another sip of my drink as the guys all start chiming in.

"No randoms."

"No celebs."

"No hookers."

Classy.

"No bunnies."

Bunnies? What are these guys into?

Nettie bounces in her seat, clapping her hands. "I've got it! Don't any of you have a sister?" There's a round of coughs, grumbles, and cleared throats. "*Okay*, so no sisters."

I can practically hear this Dateless's molars grind as he casts his buddies a killing glare. "I'm. A. Good. Guy."

Nettie bites her lip, but then something catches her attention from across the room and she's standing to go. "Hey, I gotta check in with my bride-to-be."

She turns to me, navigating carefully around the mile-long and triple-wide legs surrounding us "Just give me a minute and I'll be right back."

"I'll be here." I don't know the bride that well. I'm only at the party because another girl from their department canceled last minute and Nettie essentially dragged me out with her. The truth is, I never say yes. I never do the impulsive thing. The fun thing.

I never do any of the things that would leave my father—a man committed to career above all else— bristling with disapproval. But tonight, I'm sour over how the career I committed to has treated me. I'm hurt by his disappointment. And maybe... some petty little part of me is loving how much my father would hate this scene.

The club.

The party.

The frilly drinks.

The jocks.

The jocks he would hate most of all. I smile and snuggle back into my seat.

The guys have resumed giving Dateless a hard time. But rather than getting pissed, he shakes his head and starts to *laugh*.

It's this deep, rumbly, good-natured sound that's really kind of nice and makes me want to laugh too. After the day I've had, that's no small feat.

I look back at Dateless, catching his eyes on mine again.

He rubs a hand over the neat clip of his trimmed beard.

He really does have a nice face. Nice eyes. Nice smile. Nice laugh. Nice shoulders that stretch his fitted shirt in a pretty nice way.

Shifting in his seat to hang a nice arm over the back, he appears to be gearing up to something. I've got a fair idea what.

I hold up a hand, turning to Client Dude. "Is he?" I wave my glass toward Dateless and ask again. "Is he a *good guy*?"

Shrug. "Yeah, sure he is."

Okay then.

Downing the rest of my drink, I turn back to Dateless. "I'll go to your wedding."

Chapter 2

Harlow

Oh my God!

My eyes blink open wide and immediately slam shut beneath the harsh glare of the morning sun and a headache that's hammering through my entire body. My heart starts to race. There's no way... I didn't actually... I wouldn't... Not in a million years.

Except I'm pretty sure *I did*.

My stomach lurches and, fighting the tangle of sheets around my legs, I scramble for my phone. Check the calendar.

Oh no.

A ten-day stretch starting Thursday is labeled with one word, all caps: WEDDING.

No.

No.

Only yes. There it is, right along with a short text string that includes my name going out and a quick note of extreme gratitude coming in, along with the address of the place we're meeting for lunch today at noon.

What's not in that text string? *His name.*

This isn't good.

In fact, this is exactly the sort of thing that would have my father sneering in disgust and adding lack of responsibility and poor decision-making to his list of my shortcomings.

Ugh.

Calling Nettie isn't going to happen. I'm too embarrassed. Besides, I already know she'd tell me to cancel the lunch and wedding via text. Block his number and put out of my mind. But there's just one problem. While I don't remember Dateless's name, I do remember that he seemed like a pretty decent guy. And more than that, I remember how it felt yesterday opening my phone and being blindsided.

The least I can do is show up and tell him to his face.

Wade

"GRADY, isn't that the chick you hooked up with last night?" Axel Erikson juts his chin toward the buttoned-up brunette peering around the bar at the lunchtime crowd.

It's summer, off-season, and while the Five Hole is a hockey bar through and through, this time of year it's a pretty mellow hangout and serves a spectacular club. Plus, it's about a five-minute walk from Wagner Arena and six from my place.

I straighten, easing off my stool.

"We didn't hook up. But that's her." And truth? I'm relieved. I wasn't sure she'd show.

Axe grunts. "Wouldn't have pegged her for a bunny."

Huh?

Harlow's already walked over to the bar where O'Dwyer, another teammate, has been swiping on Tinder for the last half hour.

"She's not." This girl wasn't working for a chance to stamp another name on her Slayers bingo card. She didn't know which sport we played, got the team name wrong twice. She didn't have the skintight clothing or fuck-me hair, and the way she looked at me when the guys cleared out and it was just the two of us talking? The words *Not Interested* don't begin to cover it.

My ego flinches at the memory of her emphatic

assurance that she wasn't into me. At all. Not even a little bit.

I had to stop her after those pretty brown eyes ran over me in a slow appraisal and she stated that whole "body business" I had going wasn't her thing.

Got it. *All* six times she'd said it.

And while a square kick to the ego is never fun—for the purpose of this trip to my hometown for my brother's wedding? It works that Harlow isn't into me.

At all.

Thing is, with the ultra-conservative outfit she's rocking, I'm surprised when O'Dwyer pats the stool beside him.

Please. Like she'd ever sit down with that guy.

Time to go rescue my fake date.

"*Dude*, she just sat down."

I swallow, not appreciating Axel's cackle one bit. "I see that."

But I don't get it.

O'Dwyer's the worst. Not only did he give up the puck that cost us our playoff spot this year, but the guy's a douche. Meets and exceeds every stereotype about professional athletes there is. Acts like he's God's gift, and the way he treats women—

Harlow's pretty smile falters. The skin between her brows pulls together like something isn't quite right.

"No, fucking way," Axel mutters.

"Yeah, I see it too."

"She doesn't know which player she hooked up with last night." He turns to me, eyes narrowing. "How drunk was she?"

My shoulders slump. More than I thought. "And we *didn't* hook up."

Harlow

OKAY, there's no way this is the guy from last night.

When I walked in, the first thing I noticed was the bulk and the facial hair. Except that's as far as recognition went. I figured maybe I'd been even more tipsy than I realized though, because his reaction to my approach was *familiar*. His smile knowing. His welcome immediate, confident, and smooth... like we were old friends.

But *no way* is this *Dateless*.

Not even a barrel of bourbon would have been enough for me to agree to share a *cab* with this guy, let alone ten days in his hometown.

Time to get out. Climbing off my stool, I force a quick smile. "Well, it was nice talking with you."

Whatever-his-name-is leans back, letting his eyes roll over me in a perusal so slow and obvious I wonder if it's possible to catch an STD from a look alone.

"Nah, you don't have to take off. Whatcha thinkin', upstairs?"

I blink. "Excuse me?"

"Classy girl like you, figured you wouldn't be into the bathroom. But I'm not going back to your place for a nooner unless I can bring a friend. You don't seem the type?"

Wow, that was definitely a question. "No, but… umm… thank you?"

Taking a hurried step back, I come up short as a wide palm meets the small of my back. My breath catches, and before I even turn to check, I know. *It's him.*

"Hey, Harlow, sorry to keep you waiting."

I turn toward that warm, rumbling voice tinged with amusement, expecting— I don't even know. But not this.

Dateless… Heck, I don't remember his physical appearance being the thing that stood out about him most. I'd thought he seemed like a guy in a pinch. Genuinely nice. *Fun.* But this man, with his crystal blue eyes and built-tough body, is crazy good-looking. His hair is neatly cut and nearly as dark as mine. And while normally I'm not a fan of facial hair, the contrast of his close-trimmed beard over that rugged square jaw is… *hot.*

And so not what I go for.

Really.

Dateless crooks his finger beneath my chin, not so subtly reminding me to close my mouth.

Oh my God, this guy just had to tell me to close my mouth!

And while it seems like that might be the kind of *mortifying* a girl doesn't come back from, somehow his gruff laugh takes the sting out completely.

"I am never drinking another Snowflake Martini again." And then I'm laughing too, because this whole situation is ludicrous.

"Ehh, maybe just one less next time?"

Whoa, and that wink and smile? That explains a lot about last night.

I've completely forgotten about the guy from the bar until he wraps a hand around my arm. "Grady, get the fuck out of here with your pickup bullshit. She came on to me first."

And here's the thing. While there's something innately soothing and pleasant about this *Grady* that draws me in, I don't like having the bar guy's hand on me at all.

"Hands off, O'Dwyer," Grady growls, his voice lethally low.

The offending hand is gone before my next heartbeat.

"Bro, don't be a douche. Seriously. She's the one—"

"It was an honest mistake," I cut in, cheeks flaming. I'd really been hoping to avoid owning up to not knowing my date's name.

"She thought you were me. We've got a date."

O'Dwyer's eyes cut to me, and he mutters, "Bullshit." But he turns back in his seat and picks up his phone.

And then it's just me and Grady, who isn't really my date or even my fake date because I'm about to break things off before this madness goes any further.

This is going to be awkward.

"Want to grab a seat?" he asks, nodding toward the back of the bar where there's a second room. "It's more private. Quieter too. We can get a table and—"

"Not… upstairs?" I have to ask.

He coughs, doing a double take. Then his brows pull forward and his eyes narrow on O'Dwyer back at the bar before returning to me. "Um… no."

Tension slips from my shoulders and I nod. "A table would be great."

Shaking his head, he leads the way.

The back room is mostly empty, and he's right, quieter too. When we're seated, I open my mouth, but he speaks first. "So, I'm Wade Grady. Kind of got the feeling you might not have remembered."

"I am *so* sorry, Wade," I start, leaning forward over

the square table. "Honestly, I never drink like that, and—"

"Yeah, you might have mentioned that last night."

A server breezes by the table, and Wade checks with me before ordering us two iced teas.

This guy knows that I like mine with lemon and two sugars, and I didn't even remember his name. I'm the worst.

He's giving me a smile as genuine as I've ever seen. "But hey, don't sweat it. I mean so long as you remember my name—which is *Wade*—when you meet my mom, right?"

Ugh. It takes everything I have not to squirm in my seat.

"So actually, about that." I put some steel into my spine. "This isn't going to work."

His easy smile stays where it is, but for a blink, there's a tension around his eyes and then it's gone.

"No?" He sounds casual, calm, as he folds those big arms over the table between us and leans in. But this isn't what he wanted to hear.

I take a breath. "I got carried away last night. It had been a… bad day. And we were having a lot of fun. I just got caught up in it."

"We were. But you do remember we didn't fool around, right?"

"No, I know." I meet his eyes again. Chicken out

and glance away. "You strike me as a decent guy. Really. But last night was an anomaly. I can't go home with you. Please understand, this is about me. Not you."

"I don't know. Seems like *some* of it has to be about me."

His brow arches, tugging the corner of one side of his mouth up with it.

Geez, he's got a really nice mouth.

"No, really, it isn't." I was being rash. Reckless. "My behavior was out of character, and I feel terrible. I know you were hoping to find someone to help you out, but as much fun as we had last night—" And it *was* fun, with every second I spend across from this man, more of the night comes into focus—the surprisingly easy conversation, the jokes, the laughter. The logic that I typically apply to every situation, though? Not so much. "I wasn't thinking clearly and I shouldn't have volunteered. I'm sorry."

Wade leans back, blowing out an exaggerated breath. "See. I was just about to let you off easy, but"—he gives me a meaningful look that somehow tickles more of that unexpected laughter from me—"then you mentioned how much *fun* we had. *Again.* That's twice inside of five minutes. And Harlow, that sounds like the kind of fun we shouldn't bench quite so fast."

I cock my head, unable to resist. "Oh really?"

A nod. "Really. I get it. You're the responsible one

with the goals and priorities. You're the girl who doesn't say yes. *Ever.* I remember. And if anyone can relate to having career goals prioritized above all else, it's me."

I blink, my heart doing an uncomfortable skip hearing him voice my thoughts back to me. Heat spills into my cheeks. I can't believe I told him that stuff.

But really, it isn't any more shocking than agreeing to be his fake girlfriend.

"Here's the thing, though. At some point, you need to give yourself a break. Even if it's just a short one." He leans his forearms on the table, and my brain sort of short-circuits seeing his pale blue oxford strain around his biceps.

I've seriously never seen arms like that before.

"Come on, what could be better than a little fun that just happens to coincide with a convenient opening in your schedule when you have no other plans, obligations, or expectations you're trying to meet? It's perfect."

"Wade—" I pause, holding up a hand. "O'Dwyer called you Grady. Which do you prefer?"

Just keeping things polite, respectful, and professional.

Again with that smile. "My teammates call me Grady. But you? Wade, please."

A shiver runs through me. Time to rip off the bandage.

"*Wade*, I'm very sorry, but I'm not spending a week with a man I've barely met… no matter how much *fun* he is."

He nods. Watches me from beneath a criminally thick fringe of lashes.

And then the corner of his mouth curves.

Harlow

NINETY MINUTES LATER, I'm parked at Nettie's kitchen table, staring into her wide eyes still smudged with last night's makeup.

"Wait, what?" she croaks, but quietly since Frank is talking on the phone in the other room. "You said *yes*? Harlow, you don't *ever* say yes. To anything. No drinks with the department on Friday after work. No softball in the summer. I only got you to come out last night by threatening to bring the party to your place if you didn't… You can't say yes to a week with some *stranger*."

Which is exactly what I'd been thinking when I told him no at lunch. But then he'd started talking and… next thing, I was asking what to pack.

"This isn't some strange guy," I defend with more gusto than the situation probably merits. Definitely.

"He's one of your clients. A pro-athlete on… one of Chicago's favorite teams."

She blinks. "Jesus, Harlow. It's hockey. He plays *hockey* for the Chicago Slayers. He's a forward with a contract up for renegotiation this month. And he's not my client. He works with Leo."

Hockey. Right.

There it is.

"Even better. A contract means he needs to keep his nose clean." Why am I arguing this?

"Well, yes," she agrees slowly. "He does."

"See, he's harmless."

Nettie scoffs. "Harmless?" Her thumbs fly over her phone and she sits back. "What is this guy, six-two, 200 pounds?" She holds up a picture of Wade on the ice, a scowl cut through every feature. "Makes his living fighting it out for a puck and slamming other six-two, 200-pound dudes into the boards to do it. *Harmless* isn't really the first thing I think of."

I straighten in my seat, pushing my mug an inch to the right. I hadn't really thought of it that way. But on an instinctual level, I just don't think this guy is trouble.

He seems like fun. And like he needs a favor, bad.

Besides, "If I'm wrong and Wade turns out to be a jerk, then… favor revoked. I'll leave."

Her eyes narrow and she reaches for her coffee. "Are you serious right now?"

I take a breath and shake my head. "I know this is crazy. I know it's not me. But God, Nettie, I'm just so sick of weighing every choice I make against how it might impact my future. Whether it aligns with my goals. If it's sending the right message to the right people." *What my father will think…* "I'm so sick of always doing the right thing and never seeing the results I'm waiting for."

"It's just a matter of time before Junior fucks up. Sorry. But PHR Bank and Trust is going to want you back in that position."

I shake my head. "I don't want to wish that. And I can't count on it. But— Nettie, I'm just tired. I'm exhausted from being me, and I guess a weeklong vacation of pretending to be someone else feels like exactly what I need."

She clucks her tongue. "Are you going to tell your dad?"

I shift uncomfortably. "If he asks."

Nettie has the good grace not to point out he won't.

Chapter 3

Harlow

The men I date fit a certain mold.

They went to the right schools, have the right professions, know who my father is, and are almost as careful weighing the risk-to-reward ratio in asking me out as I am in who I say yes to.

I never have gorgeous men pressing me for inappropriate favors like this, and it's kind of exciting. Maybe that's why, against all logic, Thursday morning I'm seated at one of the Toasty Bean's sidewalk tables, waiting on Wade Grady to pick me up.

I've spent the last four days on the brink of calling the whole thing off. But then I'd get a text, email, or call from Wade showering me with "fun facts" and "miscellaneous tedium"—he lost his first tooth in a fistfight with his cousin and has to take an allergy pill when he bales hay—and I'd end up asking half a dozen more questions, most of the time laughing so hard at the answers I couldn't catch my breath. And then for the next few hours getting caught up in the idea of having ten days with this guy who's promising me fun in exchange for a fake serious relationship.

Only now, as Wade pulls up in one of those oversized white pickups, I'm pretty sure this whole thing is crazy. But what I can't understand is why I'm going through with it anyway.

"Hey, Good Girl," he calls from over the roof, hopping out to round the beast.

I catch the server's eye and tuck a few bills under my mug as Wade jogs up. He pulls one of my bags from beneath the table, grabbing the other where it rests against the geranium planter that sections off the seating. This is the first time I've seen him since our lunch and he's wearing faded Levi's and a T-shirt with a small John Deere logo on the front that smacks of country boy—though he swears he's more small-town than country—and makes me think the sundress I picked for today strikes the right balance of casual and cute to match.

"Good Girl?" I ask, trying not to get distracted by how the muscles through his chest and arms flex as he throws the strap over his shoulder.

"If the shoe fits." He nods down to the legal pad I'm tucking into the side of my tote. "Ten to one… that's filled with notes about me and you were *studying*."

So, I wasn't the only one paying attention this week. "Of course, I was studying. I'm not the kind of person who walks into a test without being completely prepared. What do you want to know? Enderson, population 7023. Home of the Tigers. Birthplace of Carl Hammond Fossy, artist, John William Paulette, inventor, and one Wade Earnest Grady—"

His bark of laughter has me grinning. "Wikipedia? Damn, you're serious about your research."

"Always."

I follow him to the truck where Wade loads my bags into the backseat and then puts a wide hand out to help me up into the passenger seat.

Once I'm in, he braces an arm at either side of the open door and squints into the midmorning sun. "Gotta admit, I wasn't sure you'd go through with it."

I give up a guilty sigh. "Neither was I."

He nods. "Well, I'm glad you did." He closes me in and jogs around the hood before climbing in himself. "This is my baby brother's wedding, and I was dreading it. I've been so focused on the bullshit I was sure I was going to have to face, I didn't think I'd be able to enjoy a minute of it. But now? The only thing I'm worrying about is whether my mom made cookies for me."

At my raised brow, he laughs. "I'm not kidding. Having you with me makes all the difference. I know you have reservations, so thank you. I mean it."

Maybe it's the whole "sports celebrity" thing, but apparently there's some expectation that he'll settle down with a nice girl from Enderson, and he doesn't want to deal with the pressure this week.

Whatever his rationale, I'm looking forward to this escape.

Wade puts the truck in gear and, merging into traffic, tells me to pick some music.

He quizzes me about school and my favorite classes and whether I'd rather have a skinned knee or a really bad hangnail.

The knee, obviously, though he'd rather the nail. Craziness.

I'm pretty sure he's keeping me talking in an effort to counteract any lingering nerves on my part. And it's mostly working, because despite us not having a lot in common at the surface, Wade is a very relatable guy.

We swap stories for a couple hours. I've got Instagram and Facebook open on my phone, digging up pictures of the people he's telling me about. Overall, I'm feeling pretty relaxed about this whole thing when he cuts me a quick look.

"So, I know it's weird that I can't go home without finding a buffer to bring with me, but I don't want you to think it's because my family's a bunch of jerks. They're pretty awesome. Nice. Loud. Welcoming." He grips the wheel with both hands. "But there's probably something we should talk about before we get there."

We've been talking since I got into the truck. "What?"

He takes a breath. Holds it. Then— "The physical stuff."

I cough, my head cranking around in a way that betrays my surprise in no small way. Nothing contained or unflappable about it. The whole instilling-confidence-through-thoughtful-reserve thing I work for in the conference room? Not happening.

And worse, I can feel the heat pushing into my cheeks as I swallow hard.

Wade cuts me another look and, seeing my reaction, blanches. "Jesus, no! Don't pull the eject handle," he says in a rush. "I just didn't want you to worry about it. I won't be all over you."

I sit back in my seat, letting go of that held breath with a sharp, "Wade."

"I'm sorry, I was—hell, I was nervous about bringing it up." He shakes his head. "Because I didn't want to spook you or anything."

I gape.

"I know," he grumbles, but that same good humor

remains in his eyes. "This is, in fact, my first rodeo when it comes to bringing fake girlfriends home."

"Okay, then what exactly does 'I won't be all over you' mean? You won't be groping my breasts or shoving your tongue down my throat in front of your parents?" I guess I'd just assumed that much. But suddenly, talking about it seems like an excellent plan. "In fact, why don't we clarify what you *will* do, just so there aren't any surprises?"

"Yeah, that's a good idea. Would you be okay with my arm around you? Not all the time, but like when we meet my parents and friends?"

His arm? "Your arm around me is fine."

"I'll try to go easy on the rest, but just kick me if I'm too much."

The rest? "What are you normally like with the girls you date?"

His head wags back and forth. "First, I don't date that many girls. I mean, date-date. Not just— Never mind."

And there it is, a rosy spot high on his cheekbone. It's kind of cute to see a big, tough hockey player embarrassed. "I think I get it."

"Yeah, well, I'm the touchy type. I like to be close. I'm a hugger. When my girlfriend's got pretty hair or a nice dress, I like to touch it. I like to hold hands. Kiss."

His brows pull together. "Not with tongue or anything, but— It doesn't matter."

"Right." And suddenly I'm thinking about Davis, my college boyfriend. How I'd reached for his hand when he came to the house for dinner, and the look he'd given me made it plenty clear hand-holding wasn't what he'd come for. Too bad for him, my father had blazed past him, phone at his ear, without so much as a second glance, and then closed himself into his office for the night. I didn't invite Davis back.

"So the men I've dated aren't generally like that. Not so outwardly affectionate, anyway. No PDA." They greet me with a kiss on the cheek when they pick me up.

Except Craig, the man I dated for two months, who never actually kissed me. Ours was a polite parting, to say the least.

Wade nods. "Cool. No PDA."

Only that subtle tightening around his eyes and mouth says *not cool*.

"Won't people notice if you aren't doing any of that? Not so much the kissing, but the other stuff."

The sound he makes is noncommittal, but I'm already imagining friends and family I shouldn't be concerned about speculating about the longevity of our relationship. Discussing how clearly not into me he is. How rigid I seem. And all the ways I must be *lacking*.

My competitive, goal-oriented side doesn't like it.

Besides, the whole point of this week is for me to get a vacation from my reality.

"That's very considerate, Wade. But you've gone to some lengths here to convince these people I'm something to you I'm not."

This time the shift of his eyes toward me is slower. "I have."

I go for a casual shrug, trying for the easy posture he always has. "So why chance failure by trying to be polite? We need to commit or why bother at all, right?"

He licks his lips. Opens his mouth and closes it again. Narrows his eyes on the road ahead and then on me, the corner of his mouth hitched the smallest degree. The suggestion's not what he was expecting.

Wade flicks the signal for the next exit. "Let's stop at the station up here."

"For gas?" The indicator shows nearly a full tank.

"I'll top her off, but maybe we just give it a trial run. See how it goes without an audience first, yeah? And if it doesn't feel right, no sweat. Every relationship is different."

I cough, straightening in my seat as heat flames up my neck and cheeks. "You—you don't think I can pull it off?"

The shake of his head is slow. "That's not what I said."

"But?"

He laughs. "Put that little arched brow away. Just… hold on." He flips the visor down and opens the vanity mirror in front of me. "What do you see?"

I look, taking inventory of the woman reflected there. Her arms are tightly crossed over her chest, lips pursed into a slight frown, and there's a buckle between eyes that are narrowed like she's studying a problem that needs to be broken down.

Honestly, I don't spend that much time in front of a mirror beyond checking to ensure I'm putting a professional image out there. That even though I'm younger than most everyone I work with, I don't come across like I am. And it's somewhat startling to see how that carefully cultivated persona might not gel with… well, really any other situation at all.

Especially one where I'm supposed to be the love interest to some touchy jock.

After a breath, I gesture toward my reflection. "I see a woman who's been a straight-A student since the sixth grade when that witch Mrs. Hall gave me a B-plus in art. A woman who performs under pressure and doesn't crack. A quick study and someone who excels at every goal she commits to." Every goal but one, that is.

I close my eyes. I see a woman who just wants to be someone else for a while.

Unraveling my arms, I smooth my features. Relax my mouth and—

"Are you seriously *practicing* smiling right now?"

I turn to Wade. "Just find the gas station. I've got this."

This guy has no idea what I'm capable of.

Chapter 4

Wade

*H*arlow has an intensity about success that's kind of scary, so no fucking way am I about to laugh at how she's *practicing* loosening up her shoulders and going for what I'm guessing is supposed to be a more casual pose.

She's not what I expected those few times I saw her at the bank.

Not by a long shot.

And yeah, I'm sort of thinking the fam isn't going to take this thing with a woman so different than any they've seen me with before as seriously as I'd like. Which is a bummer, because it would have been nice to ride this fake relationship well into next year. But even if we're nothing more than a ten-day wonder, it'll be enough to let me enjoy being home with my brother.

For now, though, it's time to see what exactly we're working with.

I pull to a stop at the first pump, leaving my hands on the wheel as I think about my approach.

"Okay, bring on the PDA. I'm ready," Harlow says, shaking out her shoulders and taking a big breath like she's prepping to jump off the high dive.

"Yeah, I see that." Maybe I've got a death wish, but this time I can't fight the smile. Damn, she's cute. "Give me a second."

She stares at me impatiently. Time to stop being a pussy.

"So here's the plan. I'm just going to talk as we go, tell you what I'm doing as I do it, and see how it plays out. You don't like it, just—"

"Should we have a safe word?" she cuts in, leaning toward me. "Something that signals we're serious and want to stop?"

I swallow and run a hand over my twitching lips. Nod. "Yeah, um, how about 'Knock it off, Wade' or maybe cutting to the chase and saying 'Stop' or 'No.' Both are instantly effective with me and might seem more natural than you casually working 'armadillo' or something into the conversation."

I've got to give her credit. Harlow doesn't look away, even when her cheeks start to flush.

"That works."

Figured it might.

"Okay, how about we start with something simple, like your hair." I sling my arm over the seatback between us and touch the dark silk I've been trying not to notice since she got in the truck.

Harlow's brows furrow again as I tease a few loose strands, looping them around my fingers before tucking them behind her ear.

Uh-huh. Yep, she's not breathing, and so much for that shoulder shimmy when she wanted to loosen up. Because now, she's straight as a stick, eyes cranked to the side as she tries to focus on my too-close hand.

Totally natural.

No one's going to suspect a thing.

Fuck.

I can see it's costing her big not to bat my hand away, and I laugh. Seriously, what else am I going to do?

How is this girl so easy to talk to while physically being wound so tight?

"What's wrong with my hair? I was going for something softer, but—"

"It's perfect, Harlow." And it is. As long as it is dark, that thick spill over her shoulder was one of the first things to catch my eye. "I'm using it as an excuse to get closer. Sure, I could tell you that there's a pretty bit of hair that's fallen free of that barrette you've got the rest clipped into, and then let you excuse yourself to fix something I like better the way it is."

She pulls back an inch. "You do?"

A lot, actually. "Sure. Which is why I'll take the opportunity to play with said pretty bit of hair myself. I get to move a little nearer"—I demonstrate, bringing my mouth close enough to her ear she'll feel the warmth of my breath, and after waiting a beat longer than strictly necessary to ensure she actually *does*, I go on—"while I tuck those rogue strands away."

And that's what I do. "Pretty."

"Thank you," she whispers, and then seeming to shake off whatever uncertainty she was feeling, she says it again, louder, with more confidence. Like she's got a point to make and she wants every last guy in the conference room to get it.

"In this case, Harlow," I murmur quietly, "version one of that thank-you works the best."

"Okay. I've got this. Do it again."

I blink at the no-nonsense dictate. I clear my throat. Mentally promise my ego it's only ten days and it's going to be okay. Then I'll find some girl who thinks I'm exactly her type with this whole "body business" and let her stroke it—my ego, I mean. Totally.

We go again. "…and I tuck it behind your ear because I'm an affectionate guy and it gives me a chance to stay close to you for just a few seconds longer."

Which I do.

She's beautiful. And the longer I stare into the deep brown of her eyes, the more I feel that power shift tipping back in my favor. Because now she's peering up at me through her thick, dark lashes, only to look away with a catch of her breath that is *way* more like it.

Ego saved!

Or so I think.

Harlow leans in just a bit too eagerly, that sort of sexy, shy thing of two-point-five seconds ago nowhere to be found.

"That was better?" She nods without waiting for me to agree, a squint of satisfaction in her eyes. "That breathy business nailed it, *right*?"

I let out a laugh and kiss my ego goodbye. "Yeah, you nailed it."

Harlow

WADE WAS RIGHT about the test run. I'm out of my element with him, but I'm a quick study. Was it strange having him touch my face and hair? Yes, it was. But was it something I could handle for a ten-day stretch? Absolutely.

Even knowing his attention is all for show, it's no hardship having a man give me his best flirt. It's the sort of thing I've never encouraged, the sort of thing I've spent more of my life shutting down than letting get in the way of my goals.

But for this week… it *is* my goal.

And I don't want anyone wondering why a man like Wade would want a woman like me.

A few miles pass with Wade drumming his thumbs over the steering wheel in time with the radio. He's relaxed, at ease. Like he figures that one practice run was plenty.

It might be. But I like to be sure.

Also, I can't stop thinking about the woman in the vanity mirror. She's not invited on this trip, and I'm going to make sure she's gone before we get to Enderson.

Wade gives me a curious smile. "What's up?"

"There's an exit coming up. Let's take it."

He stops drumming and I feel the temperature go up.

Clearing my throat, I try to sound as casual as I intend this thing to be. "This time, no telling me what you're going to do before you do it. Just act natural and let's see how it goes."

When we pull into the station, it's into a spot about halfway across the parking area rather than at the pump.

He cuts the engine and hops out. And when I open my door, he's there, flashing me that smoldering smile, eyes crinkled at the edges, mischief shining through.

"Okay, Good Girl, ready for some more practice?"

"Ready to be wowed? I'm going to kill it." Then I hold up a hand. "Wait, I know we said we weren't going to, but do you think you should try kissing me this time? Just in case?"

Wade's eyes drop to my mouth, linger for a beat that does something sort of strange to my chest. "You'd let me kiss you?"

His voice sounds deeper, each word almost deliberately placed.

"I mean… if you think it will convince whoever needs convincing. Then, yes."

"I appreciate that." His eyes shift back to mine, his smile returning. "But how about we don't pull the pin on that one unless we really need to."

"Emergency kissing only. Got it."

Wade lets out a gruff chuckle. "It's a plan."

I start to climb out of the car, but Wade's there. His big hands landing on my hips to lift me down. I'm not expecting it and go stiff for a second.

But wow.

I've never had a thing for athletes. Those oversized jocks who always seemed to take up more space than their share drove me crazy in school. Right now, though? Wade is giving me a lesson in the benefits of muscles.

"Might have to work on that one," he says with a smile.

"You're strong." I think my heart might have stopped beating, or maybe I just stopped breathing.

He winks. "Hockey player."

Catching my hand in his, he walks backward, pulling me along with him toward the store. That smile as firmly in place as the eye contact he's not giving up.

It's another novel experience. Uncomfortable and a little electric all at once.

"You want to look away. I can see it," he teases in a low, singsong voice. "Bet you can't make it all the way inside."

"Oh, I can make it inside," I assure him, my own smile rising to the challenge.

I'm not afraid of eye contact. In business, I have no qualms about meeting a man's eyes, and I can say with some degree of certainty I'm rarely the one to blink first. And never because I'm intimidated.

But with Wade, it's different. None of those business associates offered the undercurrent of smolder in their smiles that Wade Grady seems incapable of shutting down in his.

He pushes through the front door and grins. "You win." Then, when I think he's going to let my hand go, he changes the hold so our fingers are threaded together and leads me toward the coolers. "Let's grab a drink."

When we get back to the car, me with an iced tea and Wade with some jacked-up water drink, I shake my head. "I can do better."

He pulls my door open and helps me up. "You did fine. Don't get in your own head."

I scoff, waiting until he rounds the hood and climbs in on his side. "That was a seventy percent. *At best.*"

Wade's face does something weird and horror seeps into my voice. *"Sixty?"*

This time he turns to me. "Are you... *grading yourself?*"

I blink. Feel the familiar burn of embarrassment crawling up my neck and into my cheeks. My arms cross and I sit straighter. "What if I am?"

He reaches for my crossed arms, using a single finger and that smile to pry them loose. Then he leans in, again getting close enough to my ear that I can feel the teasing warmth of his breath. "That was a solid eighty-five. And with another pit stop or two, you'll be acing this."

"Sweet-talker," I say, relaxing into my seat.

"Next exit's in seven miles." He starts the truck with a wink and heads back toward the highway. "So I'm guessing you're the girl who always blew the bell curve, huh?"

I grin, not even trying to hide it. "You know it."

Chapter 5

Wade

A few hours later, I turn off on Prairie Lane and follow the gravel road back through the trees, passing the first two mailboxes before making a left at the third. The crush of gravel welcomes me even before the trees open up enough to see the house.

"Dad loves to take care of the yard. And Mom's got some pride over those flowerbeds. If you want to butter them up, that's the way to do it."

Clicking her tongue, she shoots me a withering glare. "Now I'm going to feel dirty when I compliment them. And for the record, I would have done it on my own."

Leaving the joke about *feeling dirty* untouched, I pull

in next to Walt's Ranger where the drive widens for a turnabout. When I lived at home, he and I shared a beat-up truck that didn't have privileges in the attached two-car garage, so we parked in the open space on the side.

It's empty now, but too much to hope it will stay that way.

Shit. I'm an asshole for even thinking that.

When I don't get out of the truck, Harlow touches my hand. "You sure you want to do this? Lie to your family? It's not too late to back out. Tell them I broke up with you in the driveway. Honestly, it would be fine."

I grin at her. "No way. You're stuck with me. Unless you need to bail."

Please don't need to bail.

She huffs a quiet laugh. "No quitter here."

"Okay, then." Wrapping my finger with one of those dark ribbons of silk, I give it a gentle tug. Harlow's lashes lower and she gives me the kind of coy smile that is some serious grade-A work. "They're probably already watching out the window. But once I open this door, guaranteed, we're going to have less than twenty seconds before the Gradys are all over us."

Her eyes light. "This is intense."

I nod. "So here's the game plan—"

"Not a jock here."

Maybe not, but she's got the focus of one.

"We'll check into the hotel this afternoon, which gives us some time with the family and then a good excuse to cut out for a break."

"Nice. We'll be able to address any questions that come up in private."

Harlow is all about the mission.

"Or, you know, catch a nap or a few minutes without the familial barrage of questions that's about to come raining down on you."

Yeah, my brother's the one getting married next week, but having me home for a stretch like this is an opportunity my parents don't see often. Grace and Bill will not squander it.

And the fact that I've brought a girl along?

They aren't going to want to let her go for a second.

"Will they think it's weird that we're just sitting out here?"

I laugh and lean in, kind of wishing I could kiss her because… Well, because I'm nervous as hell and it would be a really nice distraction. Or it would be if I could forget how completely not interested—not even a little bit—she is.

Instead, I bring our foreheads together and watch her lips. "This looks like I'm kissing you."

Suddenly, she pushes me back with an indignant

squawk. "We're in your parents' drive, Wade. So I can meet them for the *first time*. Seriously, there's no way I'd start making out with you before we go in."

Probably not. And then she's slipping out the passenger side door with a laugh as I reach for her hand, wanting to hold off the inevitable those few seconds more.

But no dice.

The front door opens wide and the circus comes pouring out.

Harlow

WADE'S MOM hits us first, hands shot up in the air, a peppy bounce to her step that hints at her cheerleading roots. And then she's squeezing Wade's face and pulling him down into a hug.

The second she releases him, his father whips a football at him. "Think fast."

Wade catches it without a blink and shakes his head as his father closes in to slap his shoulder and pull him in for a one-armed hug. "Still got it, kid."

When his dad steps back, he's got the ball again and drapes an arm around his wife's shoulders.

They turn to me, smiles wide, and my heart starts to pound. Because suddenly this isn't just about me filling my pathetic, empty time off with a crazy challenge that's all about having some fun. I'm not just helping Wade out with some long-standing girl trouble and communal expectations. I'm lying to his family and friends.

Why did I think this was a good idea?

The Gradys seem so sweet. Caring. Invested. Standing together with their warm eyes and smiles that match their son's, all that's missing is an apple pie.

But before the truth comes spewing out in a guilty confession, Wade is there, taking my hand with his.

"Mom, Dad, this is Harlow Richards. Harlow, these are my parents, Grace and Bill."

"Well, aren't you lovely!" his mom says as I tell them what a pleasure it is to meet them.

Several introductions follow. I offer to shake hands, get looks like I'm adorable, and then get pulled into one hug after another. Wade's brother Walt is a slightly younger, shorter version of him with a smile that's somehow even more mischievous. To hear Wade tell it, Walt is the Enderson equivalent of Nettie—the guy who can't help becoming everyone's best friend. His fiancée, Janie, is a tiny thing, all smiles and just as energetic as her soon-to-be mother-in-law. She wants to know if I can teach her to make Indian food, and as much as I wish I knew how, I have to let her down because I can't even cook it myself.

We're all heading into the house when a late model Impala pulls up the drive, passing the truck to park in a spot at the side of the garage.

Wade shifts behind me, his big hands moving to my shoulders. This has to be her, because not only can I feel the tension coming off him, but the chatter around us has gone quiet.

There's a flicker of something in Grace's eyes as they dart from the car to her son. But then Bill's stepping between us, a warm smile on his face as he waves toward the blonde climbing out with a paper bag of groceries in each arm.

"There she is. Wade, grab those groceries for Kelsey. She's been running herself ragged helping to get everything ready for this week."

"Yeah, of course." Wade presses a quick kiss to the top of my head and then jogs to the car. "Good to see you, Kels. Let me get those."

Kelsey takes a big breath, holding it in for a moment as she smiles up at him. "How are you, Wade?"

It's just a question, but there's something about her tone, the quiet delivery—like it's not for anyone but them—that catches my attention.

"I'm good, thanks," he says, leaving an extra few

inches of space between them as he takes the bag from her arms. Then when he sees that I've followed him over, he smiles and introduces us.

I slip a finger through one of his belt loops, giving it a tug like I saw Janie do with Walt. "Why don't you give me that bag and you can grab whatever's left in the trunk."

Wade

HARLOW TAKES the bag from my arms and starts walking toward the house with my mother. I could have kissed her for real right then.

I watch, kind of awed as she coos over the flowerbeds like she didn't just swoop in and stake her claim like a champ.

After a beat, I swallow and turn to face Kelsey.

She's a sweet girl, a friend as close as family since we were fifteen, a permanent fixture in my home from two years after that. I care about her. I do. But the longing in her eyes when she pulled up is the reason behind the dread gnawing at my gut every time I think about coming home.

She's not over it.

She's still waiting.

And Christ, I don't want to have this conversation again. I don't want to have to see her tears or hold her hand. And selfish asshole that I am, I don't want the guilt that goes along with her brave, stricken eyes chewing at me from the inside out every time our paths cross for the duration of our stay.

"I was surprised when your mom said you were bringing someone to the wedding." She gives me a smile packed with so much baggage I feel kind of sick. "She's not in any of your social. This is pretty new?"

I give her the smile I save for interviews after a loss. The one I don't fucking mean but gotta sell anyway. "Yes and no. She's pretty private, so we haven't been posting."

I grab the last couple of bags and Kelsey closes the car up.

We're halfway to the house when she stops. "You never bring dates home."

The front door is close, but only a dick would keep walking.

"I guess I don't." For a long time, it was because I was trying to be sensitive to Kelsey. Not make things any harder than they had to be. But after all the years, all the conversations laying it out in no uncertain terms —I don't feel that way about her—it was time for something else.

"Harlow's different." And because I really want this to be the last of the conversation, I add, "She's special."

Kelsey blinks, her next breath drawing her chin higher, spine straighter. Strong, even when it hurts.

Fuck.

"I'm happy for you."

She's not. But maybe someday she will be.

Inside, Dad and I help put the groceries away while my mom waves Harlow and Janie over to the kitchen table, telling them to ignore the mess of tule-trimmed notepads and sparkly binders littering the surface. Walt is on the phone with a couple of the guys he's got flying in for the bachelor party tomorrow night, and Kelsey's making tea.

"We're so glad you could join us this week, Harlow," Mom says, taking the eggs from my dad to load into the fridge. "I'll try not to smother you, but it's so rare Wade brings anyone home. I'm excited to get to know you."

"I've been looking forward to meeting you too."

For about the last three hours.

I close the pantry door and move into the space behind Harlow. "Yeah, but Mom, try not to run her off with seven million questions and some endless tour of photo albums, please."

Harlow's brows pop. "Don't listen to him. I'm dying to see the albums." Then, pointing to the spread of wedding madness in front of her, she quickly adds, "But only if there's time. And please, put me to work for anything you need. I'd love to help."

My mom is delighted, but Kelsey lets out a soft laugh, easing into the empty seat beside Janie. Reaching across the table, she pulls the piles closer to her.

"Oh my goodness, *no*, Harlow. You're *so* sweet to offer, but if the Gradys need anything at all, they know they can count on me."

Jesus.

Walt and Janie exchange a meaningful glance. But I'm not worried.

Harlow's not going to have her feelings hurt. She isn't going to run off.

And after what I saw in the yard when we arrived, I'm pretty sure she's going to take Kelsey's territorial stake as a personal challenge. And rise to it.

Harlow gives me an adoring smile over her shoulder. "Well, the offer stands. But I suppose there are worse things than having Wade show me around his old stomping grounds." One slender brow arches up and, cool as can be, she adds in a teasing lilt, "Maybe even a stop out at Gilman's Ridge?"

I choke as Mom and Dad let out matching barks of surprise and the blood drains from Kelsey's face.

"Dude," my brother laughs. "Of all the places, you told her about the Ridge? Classy."

The hell I told her about the Ridge. I haven't even

thought about Enderson's infamous make-out point since I graduated from high school and started banging in dorm rooms and then my own place. But I'm guessing my favorite study-bug did a little extra-credit work on her own.

I can't wait to hear what else she's dug up.

Chapter 6

Wade

I take my share of teasing over the next two hours. Kelsey excused herself not too long after we arrived, and I've been out back with Walt and Dad, just shooting the shit. Exactly like I'd hoped for. Dad wants to hear more about the endorsement deal I landed and if I'm stretching and keeping fit enough in the off-season. If any of the rumors about Baxter stepping into a coaching role are true.

For a guy whose heart broke the day I stopped throwing spirals, my dad is behind me in my hockey career one hundred percent.

Damn, it's nice to be home.

But it's almost four and I want to give Harlow a break this afternoon. Heading in, I find her sitting with my mom and Janie, checking out baby pics, all three of them shoulder to shoulder, talking a mile a minute. The sound of her laughter-laced chatter and coos almost makes me hesitant to go. My mom lifts her head and, catching me behind her, holds up the baby book for me.

"See how cute you were!"

"Potty training?" I choke, seeing not just my bare baby ass, but the twig and berries too.

The smile on Harlow's face is pure delight as I come around the couch. I take her hand and pull her up and into my side. She's not quite sure what to do with the fit, but after a beat of holding her arms stiffly at her sides, she eases into it, one arm sliding around my back.

Her body angles and her tits sort of nestle right up against my ribs.

It's not a big deal. It's just the way we're standing. Like a couple... even though we aren't one.

She didn't grab my junk.

Her tongue isn't in my ear.

But damn, that soft press of curves feels good, and it takes everything I have not to use my arm to squeeze her in even closer.

This girl is doing me a favor on the condition I'm a nice guy not out to take advantage of her while she's isolated here in the middle of freaking nowhere.

Okay, it's not quite that extreme, but I'm not going to be a douche.

So, holding my arm so it's grazing her shoulders but not pressing in, I clear my throat.

"We're going to run over to the hotel to check in and drop our bags. What's the plan for tonight?"

Mom tells us to meet back at six because half the town is coming over.

I haven't even started the engine before Harlow's twisted around in her seat, leaning into the space between us, hands clasped in a tight, neat bundle in her lap. "Tell me. That was pretty good, right?"

She's adorable.

"Oh yeah, very good." Gravel crunches under the tires as I follow the loop out. "And how the hell did you know about the Ridge?"

She scoffs, sitting back. "Research. If I take on a project, I want to be prepared."

"I'm getting that about you." I steal a glance over, admiring the light in her eyes and the glow of her cheeks. "So it wasn't too bad?"

"Not at all. You were right about your parents. They're easy to like."

It shouldn't matter, but it does. "Glad to hear it."

Harlow peppers me with questions for the next few miles into town, about me, about my family. Every time I give her an answer, I see her filing the information away. But this thing only works if it goes both ways. And hell, I just want to know more about her.

I hit my signal and pull into the drive heading up to the Picket Inn. "Once we get to our room, it's your turn on the hot seat."

I'm expecting some *bring it* attitude coming back at me, but instead I get a strained, "Our *room*? There's just one?"

Shit.

The lot's mostly empty. Parking in a spot close to the lobby, I rub the back of my neck. "I got us two *beds*. It's a suite. But—hell, I'm sorry. I guess I figured two rooms wouldn't really sell the committed serious couple thing and didn't think to check with you." I should have.

She looks out the window, back down to Main Street, and then to the doors in front of us. "Word travels fast around the *sports celebrity*?"

I laugh because there's that subtle emphasis again. From the first night in the club, any time she says it, it's like there are air quotes around it.

"Word travels fast about everything around here. But especially Bill and Grace's sons. My parents are bigger celebrities in this town than I am. Prom king and queen, varsity football and cheerleading coaches."

"And you think someone from the hotel might talk if we had separate rooms?"

No might about it. They'd definitely talk. But it doesn't matter. "I don't want to make you uncomfortable, Harlow. I can get another room." And if, against all odds, they don't have one, I'll stay in the truck. I can't stay back at my house with Kelsey there.

"No." It's like she's trying it on for size. But then she turns to me, more relaxed. "No way are we going to give up the game on day one. You caught me by surprise, but it's not like we're sharing a bed. I'm good."

I come around to help her down. "Promise you'll let me know if that changes?"

"Promise."

She hops out of the truck. Our bags are in the backseat, and when I go for the door, my hand brushes hers as she does the same.

"Sorry," we both mutter, then proceed to do the very same thing again.

She has really soft skin.

Our eyes meet, a beat passes, and then we both laugh, and hell, it just feels good.

I shake my head, this time catching her hand on purpose and guiding it away from the door. "Big, strong jock here. Let the ego have a little something, yeah?"

She rolls her eyes and steps back. "A little something? Ha. I have the feeling your ego is pretty well-fed."

"You know, you'd think that, right? But funny thing. Not so much since I met you." I throw the strap of her bag over one shoulder and mine over the other, grabbing her smaller tote in my hand. "Poor guy is starving over here."

She gives me the huff of laughter I'm going for. Then, "Wade, I'm *so* impressed with how you handle *all three* of those bags. I've never encountered such a *manly* show of strength."

Jesus, I can feel him shriveling. But she's not done.

"I might faint, I'm so overwhelmed by the testosterone in the air." Fanning herself, she asks, "If I go down, will you be able to carry me too?"

Yes. And hell, if there was any truth to her being mine, I'd already have her over my shoulder, giving that perfect round ass a spank for the mouth she's giving me. But she's not. She's doing me a favor. And not the kind that involves *going down*.

Why did she have to say it that way?

Shouldering in through the front door of the hotel, I come face-to-face with Mr. Peterman.

This guy has been giving me the stink eye since I was old enough to walk, and I've never figured out why. Or why I care. But here I am, shifting where I stand as he gives me a grizzled scowl from the check-in desk.

"Name?"

"Wade Grady." Like he doesn't know. He keeps staring, irritation evident in every breath. "Reservation through next Sunday."

He turns to a PC that's right out of the 80s and finger-pecks on the clackity keyboard. Snorts. "A *suite*."

Beside me, I swear I catch Harlow's shoulders give a shake.

Glad she thinks this is funny.

"Yes, sir. Also, we don't need anyone in to make up the room this week."

There's another stare that has me feeling guilty. For what, I don't even know. But the last thing I need is Marcy or Nadine, if they're still working housekeeping here, to let it slip that a certain couple isn't sharing a bed.

He hands us our key cards and, with a short huff, returns to the office.

Once we're in the elevator, Harlow turns to me, barely suppressed laughter playing at her lips. "*What was that?*"

I smile. "Right? I've been telling my parents he hates me since I was a kid and they're always like, 'No way, Wade.'"

There's a sort of unhealthy shimmy when the car reaches the third floor that has my hand moving to Harlow's back. But then the doors open and we're faced with a drab hallway that was probably intended to be sunny but isn't.

We're the last door on the left. And when I swipe our key card, I'm relieved to see that as dated as much of the hotel is, the room is clean and smells fresh and would probably feel plenty big if I was standing in it with anyone other than the woman beside me.

I set the bags down, eyes landing on a pull-out sofa I'm betting hasn't been replaced since I was born.

Damn. Good thing it's off season.

Harlow

THE BEDROOM DOESN'T HAVE a door, but on the upside there is a fully equipped bathroom that does. So I call it a win even if things get a bit weird once we start trying to give each other some privacy in a space that simply isn't about it.

I hear Wade opening his bag. Then the expulsion of a breath that's distinctly masculine. The creak and groan of the couch that's supposed to be his bed.

His muttered curse.

"I take you to the nicest places, huh?" he says from the other room, using a voice that's probably quieter than when it was just the two of us in his truck.

"Bed's not bad," I say, giving it a tentative bounce and then lying back on it.

"Yeah? Watch out if I start putting moves on you."

I roll my eyes. "Plotting to get off the pull-out already?"

Even from the next room, there's something about his laugh. And then I'm kind of wondering what an actual move from Wade would look like and how many of the girls in Enderson already know.

I roll to my side, stretched out along the mattress. "So, Kelsey?"

"Yeah, Kelsey." A beat passes but then he clears his throat. "We used to be pretty good friends."

I wait. Trying to imagine the past between her and Wade. When he told me about her, he'd been pretty vague, just mentioning she lived at his house. But the way she behaves around him says there must have been something.

There's another deep, protesting groan from the couch. And then Wade's standing in the doorway. One solid shoulder propped against the frame. "She's a good girl. Really."

"She's in love with you."

There's a flash of pain in his eyes as he rubs the back of his neck. "I want to tell you that's not it, but hell, I don't know. Maybe it's love. If it is, that's nothing I want to fall into."

Wade seems like such an open, lighthearted guy. It's hard to imagine him closing himself off to anything. "When did things end between you?"

He huffs a short laugh. "High school, junior year. About thirty seconds after it started." And then he's shaking his head. "It was so stupid. We were at my buddy's party. I'd just broken up with my girlfriend and I was drunk enough that all I wanted was to find an empty bedroom and clock out until the next day. But then she was there too, coming to check on me. A little drunk herself. Didn't want to go home, so she crawled in with me."

Ahh. "You slept together?"

If I were a real girlfriend, I'd probably have liked to know that before walking in blind. Lucky for Wade, I take the *fake* part of our relationship very seriously.

"Slept together in the literal sense of the word. But… sometime during the night, we must have started fooling around some. Hell, I barely remember how it started. Just the moment when I realized it had and it was Kelsey. She deserved better than some drunk dickhead. So we stopped, thank fuck. But ever since…"

He blows out a long breath and moves to the far corner of the mattress to sit. "It doesn't matter how many times I tell her it isn't happening. I've tried to be nice. Hell, I've tried to be less nice. But every time I see her, it's still there. The hope and then the hurt. And it guts me, because while I don't feel about Kelsey the way she feels about me, I care about her a hell of a lot."

Oh man. Wade is a *really* good guy.

"How long has she been living at your house? She seems pretty close with your family."

He laughs but there isn't any humor to it. "Since before we graduated. Her home life wasn't ideal. My mom's the high school cheerleading coach, and she and Kelsey bonded early on. Somehow she found out about the situation at home, and when things got really bad, Mom just moved her into our spare room. I'm glad my family could be there for her when her own wasn't. But—"

"It makes things tricky when you come home. Does your family know how it is?" But even as I ask, I remember those nervous glances and what Wade told me before the trip. That the whole town was waiting for him to come home and marry a girl from Enderson. I hadn't realized they'd actually picked her out already. "Never mind. Of course they do."

"Pretty safe to say that everyone knows how it is. Or at least they know how Kelsey feels. It's been this *Will They, Won't They* game since sophomore year. Everyone waiting for it to happen. Setting us up, pairing us off… scheming ways to get us alone. Totally ignoring the fact that I was not interested." He gives me one of those shrugs like it's no big deal, but I wouldn't be here if it wasn't. "Last time I was home, my dad was 'working on her car' and I became her ride to work at the courthouse each day… and her lift into the city an hour away that weekend."

"Wow. Your own family?"

"That's nothing. My mom left us at the high school together after practices once. Drove right off without us so we had to walk together. Strangely, no friends available to pick us up either. Social blowing up so bad for the rest of the night with everyone asking what happened, I was ready to turn off my account." He shakes his head. "But it's the guilt that gets me, you know? I don't want to be an asshole, but I don't want her wasting her life waiting for something that will never happen."

"Honestly, I can't even imagine." My life leans so far in the other direction, I wouldn't even know where to begin trying to explain it to someone like Wade. "So what happens when you've brought dates home in the past? Everyone just backs off?"

Wade laughs. "So we're clear here before I answer, I'm not some stunted emotional moron. I've had girlfriends. In high school and college. But since then, girls haven't really been the priority, so my relationships have been more"—he pauses and clears his throat—"casual."

Translation: No room for someone to catch expectations.

He gives me the side-eye. "Regardless, I've never brought a girl back with me. I just—hell, maybe I figured they weren't serious enough for what it would cost Kelsey."

"But this time?"

"It's my baby brother's wedding. Mostly, I just wanted to be able to spend some time with the guy without finding myself accidentally marooned in a field overnight with Kelsey. I don't want to be having the same conversations with her this trip I do every other." Making a fist, he presses his knuckles into the bed and then stands. "And hell, maybe I was hoping bringing someone home with me would be enough for her to finally let go."

Chapter 7

Wade

When we get to my parents' place at six, the drive is already filled with cars and there's music coming from around back.

I have a bottle of bourbon for my dad, and Harlow's got some fancy box of chocolates that my mom will swoon over, for sure. We follow the flagstone path around the side and find the patio crowded with the outdoor set I got them for their anniversary last year, three other tables that I'm guessing came from the neighbors, and an arsenal of folding chairs that extend well into the grass.

Harlow takes my hand, and I point out Janie's parents and her two older sisters and their families. I recognize a few guys my brother hung out with in high school, but there's also a handful of people I don't recognize at all. In Enderson, that doesn't happen too often, so they've got to be his buddies from college.

Harlow says everyone's names back when she meets them, and I can't resist the urge to tease. "So you remember all *their* names but not mine?"

Her cheeks turn a pretty shade of pink. "I remember your name *now*."

Small miracles. "And my ego thanks you."

It's going to need mouth-to-mouth after this week.

Mom sees us and waves us over with that big smile she's always had whether I was running off the field, out of the rink, or in from the rain on any given day.

It's good to be home.

"Welcome back!" She pulls us both in for a hug, but the quick pats on the back tell me she's running on all cylinders. "How was the hotel? It's been years since I've been inside."

"It's perfect," Harlow answers at the same time I say, "Pretty sure it hasn't been updated in that long either. The pull-out is jacked—"

I cut off as Harlow grips my hand with bone-crushing strength. My mom's brows knit into a tiny stitch.

Shit!

Mom swats my shoulder, rolling her eyes. "Okaaaay, Wade. Thank you for trying to protect me, but I didn't fall off the turnip truck yesterday. The pull-out? Please."

She chuckles some more, like it's all a big joke.

And then she's towing us into the crowd where everyone wants to say hello, talk about the varsity football team coming up this year, and ask Harlow what she thinks of our town. With the bachelor and bachelorette parties tomorrow night, the energy is high and, pretty soon, I'm going one way while Harlow casts me a wink over her shoulder as Janie and my mom lead her another.

I try to keep an eye on her, make sure she isn't getting overwhelmed. But every time I catch sight of her, she's smiling wider than she was before. Her laughter's freer. And hell, she's more relaxed in this party full of strangers than she was when it was just the two of us with a room to ourselves at the Five Hole.

Relaxed looks good on her, but I try not to get caught up in it.

We've got more than a week of faking it ahead of us. I can't afford to screw things up with this girl just because she's got the kind of laugh that—

"Harlow seems nice," Kelsey says from behind me.

Jesus. That fast, and every muscle down my spine is knotted tight. "Sorry, didn't see you before." I clear my throat. "But yeah, very."

She steps into my side. Her arms are crossed, so

there's nothing overt about the way that she's touching me. It's just her shoulder making contact with my arm. Something you'd expect from old friends, maybe.

Only with Kelsey, that's never all it is.

"You're both staying at the hotel?"

Here it comes. "Yep. All checked in."

A nod, and she turns away. But not before I see the flash of hurt.

Damn it.

"You could have stayed here. In your own room."

No. I couldn't. Not with a single wall between her and me. Not after last time. And not a discussion I'm having again now.

I give her a quick pat on the back and head over to my brother.

Harlow

WADE MAKES A PRETTY decent fake date. No matter how many times we get pulled away during the evening, he always finds his way back. Dropping a kiss at my cheek and asking how things are going as he slides an arm around my lower back. Joining whatever conversation I'm caught up in and somehow finding a way to tease and flirt more laughter out of me than I've given up in the last year. Maybe ever.

He's sweet and fun, and the way he loves his family? It kind of melts my heart. I can't even imagine what growing up like this would have been like.

For my part, I remember his name, welcome those shows of attention like a champ, and add my own bit of physical fiction when I can. My signature move is the center-chest pat. I saw Janie doing it with Walt earlier, and I liked the sweetly affectionate quality of it. It's not like I'm feeling up his pecs or abs, or patting his ass—which I also saw Janie do.

We stay at the Gradys' until close to eleven. It practically takes swearing on a stack of bibles, but I finally convince Grace I'm not just being polite and would love to help. So next week, I'll be joining her in making cookies for the dessert table and some last-minute setup while Wade handles his best-man duties and some manual labor at the hobby farm where the wedding and reception are being held. It's perfect.

I swan back into the kitchen where Wade is drying dishes with a white cloth he flips over his shoulder at my approach.

"See this?" I wave my list like a victory flag.

Setting a platter aside, he rounds the island and takes it from my hand. "Look at your bad self."

Taking my list back, I lean against the counter and

fan myself with the skinny sheet of paper with the header "From the desk of Grace Grady."

"I'm killing it."

"Yeah, you are." His smile is wide and warm as he props a hip on the counter beside me. "What's it going to take to lock down repeat performances for say… the next twenty years? I'm getting the sense my parents won't let me in the front door next time if I don't have you by my side."

It's tempting. Not just because I'm riding the high of tonight's success—though I absolutely am. Or because Wade is the kind of easy fun I never expected to be having. But because my family, what there is of it, is *nothing* like this.

I've seen my father laugh before, but only in the context of a competitor's misstep. Jokes are beneath him. And the landmines of the past are too vast and varied to tread near.

There's an appeal to feeling like you're a part of a whole instead of knowing you're just another satellite orbiting an entity bigger than yourself.

But what I'm a part of here isn't real. And no matter how nice having Grace Grady fuss over me feels or how welcoming his family is… none of it is mine.

"Sorry, Sport. You're a good guy, but I've penciled in a fake breakup for about a week before your next trip home."

"Doomed from the start." His smile grows wider. "But we'll always have Enderson?"

This guy is too much. "Yes, we'll always have Enderson."

His eyes linger on mine before finally shifting away… and freezing. "Oh, hey, Kels."

She's standing in the doorway I walked through only the moment before. I quickly replay our exchange, inwardly cringing. Even if she heard, it might sound like nonsense. A couple teasing each other, nothing more.

"Sorry to interrupt." Her hands flutter to her chest. "I was just thinking it's getting awfully late. Why don't you let me make up the couch for Harlow so you don't have to drive?"

Wade catches my hand in the firm grasp of his, pulling me in front of him and doing that thing where our fingers are still threaded together when he wraps his arms around me from behind. "Thanks for the offer, but we're good. I haven't been drinking and it's less than ten minutes to the hotel."

"But the roads are dark, and you haven't been home in a while and—"

"I'm fine, Kelsey," he says, his tone hard.

She gives him a short nod but somehow manages to avoid meeting my eyes even once. It's not exactly a snub, but real or not, it feels weird to be on the receiving end of a stranger's animosity.

After finding Wade's parents to say good night, we make our way out front. Wade holds my hand the whole way.

"Almost done." When we get to the truck, he doesn't open the door. "Remember how I said it would look like I was kissing you when we first got here?"

"I remember."

Wade draws me in front of him, positioning me so I'm resting against the cool metal.

Pushing to my toes, I try to peek past his shoulder. He's too tall. Too broad. "Do you think she's watching?"

"I know she is." With a short laugh, he angles his body, giving me a quick glimpse of the house before moving back into my space. It was just long enough to see the silhouette of a woman at the window.

"I feel bad for her but, Wade, that's kind of creepy."

"Try waking up to her slipping into your bed. Naked. And I'm not talking about back in high school."

"What? *Here?*" I try to peek past him again, only this time it's outrage more than curiosity.

He shakes his head, nudging me back against the truck. "You see why I needed the date?"

"I guess I do. But, Wade, that's not okay. Did you tell your mom?"

The smacked expression on his face is... I don't even know what to make of it.

"Seriously, the fact that you think I'm tattling to my mother—" He rubs a big hand over his jaw. "Where did I go wrong with you? Was it something I said? Something I did? My shirt, my hair?"

"What?" My hands fly up between us. "Grace just seems like a really good mom. And she's the one who invited Kelsey to move in. I don't know."

"I was twenty-four years old!" He's half yelling at me, half laughing, and I can't tear my eyes away from that openmouthed smile. His head drops forward for a beat. "Harlow, I've never met a woman so completely underwhelmed by me. And I know this whole 'body business' doesn't do it for you, but what the heck? Pro-athlete. Graduated with honors from a well-respected school—and because I know you're thinking, as an athlete, I didn't have to earn those grades the way the *real students* did, let me tell you you're wrong. I busted my ass for every one."

I believe him.

I might have been harboring some unfair stereotypes about jocks when we met, but it didn't take more than one conversation to set me straight. This is a man who *tries*.

Though why he tries so hard with me, I don't know.

"What do you care what I think, anyway?"

He considers and then gives me an easy shrug. "Don't know. But I do."

That easy admission warms my chest more than it probably should, and I don't quite know how to respond, so I circle back to the issue at hand.

"Kelsey. Assuming she's still watching—" Again I go for a peek, and again Wade reins me back in.

"Trust me. She is."

"Okay, so what do I do here?"

He stares at me through the darkness. "Maybe put your hands on my shoulders or, hell, you don't have to do anything, really. Just let me lean into your personal space for a minute, if that's okay."

My hands move to his shoulders, resting lightly over the hard, layered muscles. "It is."

Then, slowly, he lowers his head, bringing his brow to touch mine as he gently cups my cheek.

Staring up into the shadows of his face while he's touching me feels different. And even though we've been faking our way through this whole day, right now I feel inexplicably nervous.

"That's a nice touch with your hand."

Another short laugh, but this one is warm against my cheek. "My grandma used to watch soaps when I was a kid. I remember her saying the actors put their hands up like that so you couldn't see if they were really kissing."

This time the laugh is mine, and I pull back to meet his eyes. "You're soap-opera kissing me?"

"Only a little." He winks, that panty-melting smile flashing through the darkness. "If I were giving you the serious soap treatment, it would be hands roaming all over the PG parts of your body. Lots of back, arms, neck, and hair."

"Wade... are you sure it was your *grandma* watching?"

"Sorry, Good Girl," he murmurs so close to my ear, chills streak down my skin. "That information is above your paygrade."

"Mmm... saving the good stuff for a *real* girlfriend. I see how it is."

Wade starts to step back, an affectionate smile on his face when I catch him by the shirt and pull him back in for one more fake kiss. "Like we can't quite get enough, right?"

He grins down at me. "You're a pretty great fake date, Harlow."

"Told you I would be."

"Yeah, you did. Let's get back to the hotel."

Chapter 8

Wade

It's barely after six and I'm pretty sure my back is never going to forgive me if I don't get out of this crappy pull-out bed. Not the best night's sleep ever, and I'm kicking myself for not making plans before we knocked off. We aren't due back at my parents' until lunch, but I have no idea what that means for the woman in the next room.

If she's the kind to sleep in, I feel like I owe it to her to let her.

That said, the quarter-inch I moved had the springs groaning beneath me. *Shit.*

I try again, going for a quick roll, thinking if I move fast there'll only be the one noise and then I can creep out quietly. Not the case. This fucker wails like some jungle animal being dragged to its death, and I've barely swung my feet to the floor.

A soft laugh comes from the next room. "I'm awake. Just put it out of its misery and get up."

"Sorry. I didn't mean to wake you." Rubbing a hand over my face, I push to my feet.

Jesus, it's loud.

I walk into Harlow's room where she's sitting up in bed with the sheet covering her legs. She's wearing a pink, short-sleeved pajama set with white piping and buttons down the front that really shouldn't be as sexy as it is. But maybe it's her slightly rumpled hair or how she's even prettier without a lick of makeup.

Whatever it is, I need to forget about it before she notices that I'm standing like a creeper at the end of her bed. I clear my throat. "Give me two minutes and I'll be out of here and you can sleep as long as you like."

She waves me off. "I'm good. Early riser. I was texting with Nettie."

"Letting her know I'm not a serial killer? Maybe we should snap a proof-of-life selfie."

"I was actually thinking about sneaking out for a run. I can get one then."

I perk up. "You run? That's what I was heading out for. We could go together if you want? I can do an easy one today. Maybe show you around?"

Her sleepy eyes light, and I have a wholly inappropriate flash of what it would be like to see her peering up at me from the pillow.

Not cool, creeper.

Thankfully, Harlow doesn't follow my train of thought and bounces out of bed, ducking into the bathroom before I have a chance to beat her there. Through the paper-thin door, she calls out, "Don't blow off your workout on my account. I don't want to slow you down."

"It's one day," I assure her. "It'll be a nice break. Fun."

"NO, really, Wade, don't hold back on my account," Harlow teases, jogging backward in front of me as we close out the sixth mile of a run I was expecting to be more about leisure and less about this ego-crushing good girl giving me a lesson.

"Ha-ha," I say, chasing her down the path through the wooded park. Yeah, I could take her in a race... I think. I could outlast her... probably. But it wouldn't be easy. And not only is that unexpected, but it's pretty damn hot too.

As hot as the black running shorts and matching tank that's cut like the white sports bra she's wearing beneath. As hot as the long braid that's draped over her shoulder and dipping into the valley between her breasts.

Don't gawk, perv.

I clear my throat, watching her face and not the sweat-slicked expanse of her golden-brown skin. "You got me. I'm the dickhead underestimating you. Again. You're a badass."

Her smile cranks up, and I find my own rising to match it.

"You'll learn. I'd like to think, eventually, everyone will."

The way she says it, quietly, more to herself than to me, makes me wonder how often and how badly she's sold short.

It's a mistake I won't make again.

The path splits ahead, but we bypass the loop around the lake for the one leading down to a pebble beach. Slowing to a walk, I wipe the sweat from my brow with the back of my arm.

"And your reward for spanking me on this morning's run. Behold, Lake Ridley."

"It's beautiful here," she says, her skin flushed from exertion, those burnt-umber eyes lighting up as she takes in one of Enderson's best views.

"It is."

She is. She's beautiful. Sharp. Driven. Funny. Competitive. And unexpected.

So unexpected.

I think that's my favorite part.

"Is this where you ran when you were growing up?" She puts her hands on her hips and bends at the waist before straightening up and balancing on one leg to stretch out the toned muscles of the other.

I laugh, shaking my head. "Nah. I ran for football, but only where they told me to. How long, how far. Never anything more. Same with hockey. It wasn't until I was coming home on breaks from college that I started running out here."

When I started needing excuse after excuse to get out of the house.

Harlow cuts me one of her sidelong looks, and I have to remind myself that we're not in public so pulling her into my chest isn't on the table. And my T-shirt's soaked through with sweat, so... gross.

"What?"

"Tell me about the football. What happened there?"

I grin and grab her hand, leading her down to the shore where the water laps gently against the stretch of small stones nestled between piled boulders at either side. Guiding her around the rocky bend, we come to the sheared-off slab of a boulder high-schoolers have been calling "the bed" since my parents were kids. Probably longer.

I help her up and then hoist myself onto the level top, leaving a few inches between us. The sun glitters gold on the lake in front of us, and I lean back on my arms, letting the stone cool my overheated body.

"So basically, no one saw the hockey thing happening. It was sort of an accident and one I'm pretty sure my dad hasn't forgiven himself for yet."

Harlow laughs and leans back, mirroring my pose. "This sounds good."

"Yeah, local football legend raises hockey pro. Family can't live down the shame."

"Okay, so tell me about it. But keep in mind I don't speak jock, so you'll have to dumb it down for me."

"Ha, pretty sure I don't have to dumb down anything for you." But I do need to keep my eyes off that bare stretch of skin between her shorts and tank. Damn. "Here's the short version. I was athletic, energetic. You know how it is with kids. They do all those tyke-level sports, getting a taste of everything."

She wrinkles her nose. "My father isn't really into sports. I played the piano and clarinet."

And her mom passed away when she was young. I feel like an ass.

"Well, I was a kid who took to all of it. Mostly because I had an overload of energy and my mom was willing to run all over Enderson to help me burn it off. But the expectation was always that I'd play football like my dad. Only problem was, football's a fall sport and once it ended, I was climbing the walls."

"Hockey's a winter sport?"

I smile. "Yeah, it is. There are other winter sports too. Thing is, the basketball coach made the mistake of asking my mom out in high school."

Harlow's eyes go wide. "He didn't dare!"

"Right? Needless to say, there was no way in hell William Grady's kid was shooting hoops."

"Why not something else?"

"Mom's favorite cousin played hockey. So, I hit the ice."

"And that was the day the football died?"

"Hardly. I played both sports into high school. My dad still thinks I could have gone all the way with football."

She turns to me, squinting in the morning light. "You don't think so?"

"Nah. I didn't want it with football the way I did with hockey. I had a lot of the components you need to win. But if it's more than the win you're after, you have to *want* it. You have to want it more than anything else, because there's a cost to getting it, and there's only the one way that payoff works out."

I can see her absorbing what I just told her. Weighing it in a way I don't see with most people.

"Was it hard to choose?" Her voice is quiet, thoughtful. "Knowing what your dad wanted for you wasn't what you wanted?"

"It was brutal. Before I told him was the worst. There were months of that gnawing ache in my gut when I knew I was going to let him down."

She nods, looking off into the distance. "I know that feeling."

"I hung on to that longer than I should have. And then one night after a meatloaf dinner, I finally sacked up and spit it out. He just stared at me for what felt like an eternity. My mom let out this horrified squeak and, yeah. That was a rough summer."

She's watching me intently now. Her eyes soft and curious. "But it was worth it? You're happy? No regrets?"

It takes me a minute to answer. No one asks me that. Ever.

I'm playing in the NHL. It's a dream not many realize. But it comes with sacrifices that start the second you realize you have to put it before everything else, and that might continue well past the last time you step off the ice.

But none of that changes my answer.

"I'm happy. It's been a long time coming, but I'm

finally where I wanted to be." Or I will be once the contracts are signed. "And as to regrets? Only that I wish my dream hadn't come at the cost of my dad's."

"I get it." She smiles again. "But even if he was disappointed at first, that man is so proud of you now. No matter how he teases you, I don't think even he would change a thing."

I like that she sees it. That she understands. I like that she's sitting on "the bed" with me in one of my favorite spots in my hometown.

Hell, I like her. Period.

Chapter 9

Harlow

I wasn't sure about crashing my second bachelorette party in as many weeks, but Janie wouldn't hear of me skipping out. And now that I'm back at the hotel, tipsy from too many sugary drinks and still giggling thinking about the "police officer" who showed up at her sister's house during dinner, I am so glad I went.

Wade and I texted a few times early on in the evening, but then Grace caught me and commandeered my phone, texting her son in no uncertain terms that this was a girls' night and he could have me back when the party was over. She's feisty and so much fun.

Dressed for bed but still a little wound up, I check my phone wondering if Walt had as much fun at his party as his bride-to-be had at hers and if all Wade's plans for the night turned out the way he'd hoped.

I wonder if he'll be back before I go to sleep.

If we'll talk through the wall the way we did the night before. I kind of hope so, because it was surprisingly nice getting drowsy to the sound of his voice.

He has a really nice voice.

Okay, definitely still tipsy.

The door to our suite unlocks and I sit up, a frisson of excitement sweeping over me. After a quick knock, Wade lets himself in and—

"Whoa, are you okay?" I ask, stumbling out of bed as I take in the train wreck that is my fake boyfriend. His hair is standing in total disarray, there are lipstick smudges on his face, and his button-down shirt is hanging open… no buttons to be found.

Wade throws the slide lock and slumps back against the door with a long breath. Tired eyes meet mine, and when he brings up his hand in the universal stop signal, I see his sleeve is literally torn at the cuff.

"I swear, it's not what it looks like."

"It looks like…" Like maybe someone needs to call the real police.

"Someone told the *dancer* at the club I was a hockey player."

Huh? And then it hits me.

Ooh… The "sports celebrity" thing is *real*.

"She's a Slayers fan? Or just a really hardcore Wade Grady fan?" I whisper, trying to shut down the pinch of jealousy I'm experiencing at the sight of all that lipstick.

Wade lets out a dry laugh. "She'd probably never even heard my name before. I only started getting real ice time in the games this past season. But knowing I'm a pro, sometimes people get caught up in it." His eyes cut to mine, his smile coming back online. "Present company excluded."

"No, I'm impressed. I am." Fine, not so much about the sports. But in other ways.

"You're killing me, Harlow." He pushes off the door and walks through to my room with a weary laugh. "I want you to know, this isn't what I was going for. I asked her to back off. Tried to be *nice*. Told her I had a girlfriend."

At my shocked cough, he shakes his head. "What? For the purposes of this week, *I do*. And so we're clear, I would never disrespect the woman I was with by flirting up or encouraging this kind of crazy shit." He holds up his arm, examining the torn fabric, and mutters a curse.

Then he's shouldering out of his shirt, and I'm trying not to notice the muscles across his chest flexing and shifting as he frees one powerful arm and then the other.

"I really appreciate that." I do. "But, um…"

His head comes up. "Yeah."

I can barely say it out loud. "I put… twenty dollars in Officer Johnson's man thong thing."

Wade blinks. Shakes his head and blinks again before barking out a laugh so loud I'm afraid he'll wake the whole hotel.

"I feel bad," I gasp, laughing too. Okay, not that bad. "You were such a good fake boyfriend while I'm this, this *tart*."

When he finally catches his breath, he sits back on the desk across from the bed. "Hey, how'd it go with the bachelorette party anyway? You girls have fun?"

I start to answer but, with the way his arms are braced at his sides with those massive legs stretched out in front of him, I'm getting lost in the deep-cut ridges of his abdominal muscles.

So many.

He asked me about the party. Right.

It takes me a second to get my eyes up past his neck, and when I do, I find Wade watching me with one raised brow and a smile that says I'm so busted.

I sigh, holding up my hands. "Okay, I'm impressed. For real."

He grins. *"Finally."*

Taking a last look at the shirt, he tosses the wrecked garment in the bin beneath him. "The party, Harlow."

Yes. Right.

"It was so much fun. Thank you for the nudge, by

the way. I would have been fine with a night here in the room, though. So if anything comes up that you need to do on your own, don't worry about me. I mean that. But tonight was a really good time, and I'm glad I got to go."

"Just tell me Janie's stripper didn't get as handsy as ours did. If my brother's taking a swing at me tomorrow, I want to be prepared for it."

"He didn't." I laugh and, peering up at him, get caught in that smile. "No offense to Walt, because he seems like a really nice guy. But I'm having trouble imagining *him* coming after *you*."

Wade has several inches on his brother and a couple dozen pounds of muscle, at least. The bulk of which I'm still getting an eyeful of.

"If you'd seen us growing up, you wouldn't doubt it. That little fucker fought dirty."

And now I'm imagining the two boys Grace showed me picture after smiling, innocent picture of going after each other. When I finally stop laughing, Wade's eyes are still on me.

And I like it. I like the way he smiles at me and the way he laughs with me and the way he looks at me like he *likes* me.

Tracing a square in the pattern of the bedspread, I put my thoughts back on track. "Okay, so dirty fighter aside. What reason would Walt have to come after you?"

"I might have helped Janie's mom out with the entertainment."

My jaw drops. "*You* hired Officer Dwayne DeLong-Johnson? That is the funniest thing I've ever heard. But it definitely makes more sense than Mrs. Hamilton scouring the exotic dancer listings on her own. FYI, she couldn't stop giggling the entire time he was there. Her face was tomato red, but she was *delighted*."

Pushing off the desk, that hooked grin in place, he heads for the bathroom. "Nice. I'm glad Janie had a good time."

He leaves the door open and turns on the sink, so I follow him back and prop a shoulder in the doorway. "Janie did too, but I was talking about her mom. *And yours*."

Rocking back on his heels, he cackles. "Tell me there are pictures."

"Oh, there are pictures, all right. I'm pretty sure Janie has video too. Play your cards right, and maybe she'll share them."

Still grinning, he runs a washcloth under the tap, soaping it up before he goes after the lipstick marring his jaw and forehead.

Catching sight of a few pink smears he probably can't

see, I step into the room, take another washcloth from the rack, and reach around Wade to get it wet. After the last two days, I've gotten so used to intentionally touching when we have an audience, I don't even think about the fact that my hand is pressed to the bare skin of his side until I look up and find him watching me in the mirror.

"Sorry," I breathe out, pulling my hand free. Suddenly, the laughter is gone, leaving only the awareness of how small this room is and how close we're standing.

"There's some on your neck and back too… If you want me to get them."

He nods, and I try to focus on wiping away the evidence of some other woman on him, but my gaze keeps slipping back to the mirror. To the too-blue eyes still watching mine, impossible to read.

I want to say something. Break the silence. But that easy conversation between us feels further out of reach as the seconds stretch.

"There, you're all cleaned up," I finally manage, still clutching the washcloth.

Wade turns, his big body swallowing up the space in the small bathroom in a way it hadn't when his back was turned. He reaches for a bit of my hair like he did at the gas station—God, was that only yesterday?—and wraps it around his finger before smoothing it back over my ear.

The air feels thin, warm.

His knuckles graze that sensitive skin along my neck.

Forget thin. The air is gone.

Or maybe I'm just holding my breath. His brows pull forward, those blue-sky eyes turning midnight as they track the path his fingers just followed, then slowly shift back to mine.

Something cold splatters against the top of my foot, shocking the air back into my lungs on a gasp.

I'm clutching the wet cloth in my hands hard enough to wring the liquid from it.

When I look back to Wade, whatever I thought I saw is gone and all that's left is the easy smile.

He takes the washcloth from me, setting it at the back of the sink. Then wrapping his hands around my shoulders in a gentle hold, he guides me backward until I'm outside the bathroom. "Thanks for getting the lipstick off. Hit the sack and I'll try to be quiet when I'm done showering."

And then he closes the door.

Chapter 10

Wade

It's the crack of dawn and I can't stop thinking about Harlow. About standing in that bathroom last night with her fingertips burning into the bare skin of my side and those deep brown eyes peering up into mine.

Good thing she turned away when she did, because I was about to do something epically stupid. And I don't want to be that guy for her.

I want to be a good guy. Not the jerk who convinced her to help me out, only to pay her back by putting moves on her two days into a ten-day favor.

Thing is, it would be a hell of a lot easier to be good if every now and then she didn't look like she might be thinking something bad.

Keyword there being *might*. As in, also *might not*.

Outside of this week, I'm not a guy who holds back, waiting to see how things play out. I'm a guy who goes after what I want.

The girl, the game, the puck. Whatever it is. I don't mess around.

If Harlow had been giving me those eyes under any circumstances other than these, I would have had my mouth on hers within a blink. I would have—

Nope.

I'm not going to be the douche lying here getting hard thinking about her mouth and all the ways I want to play with it. What those lush lips might taste like. How soft and sweet they'd be parting beneath mine. What it would be like wrapping my hand in the thick silk of her hair and backing her up to the bathroom wall—no, the *shower wall*—while foamy soap slips between us, trailing over her tits and down to her—

Fuck! Don't think about her like that when she's one freaking Saltine-cracker-thin wall away.

I take a deep breath, concentrating on the three springs grating against my spine, hip, and shoulder instead of shower scenarios that might have been until I think I might be facing a career-ending injury if I don't move.

I roll to my side, cringing at the screech of the springs beneath me.

And there's the laugh.

"Sorry 'bout that."

"I was already awake. Just giving you some extra sleep if you needed it."

"Nah, I'm set." Total lie. I could probably use about six more hours. But that's not happening now. And not just because of the bed.

There's some rustling from the other side of the wall and then Harlow's standing in the open arch between our rooms.

Jesus, she's beautiful. That inky hair falling around her shoulders in sleep-mussed sexiness. Her golden skin and bottomless eyes devoid of any makeup. And those conservative button-down PJs clinging to her curves in a way that has me pressing the heels of my hands into my eyes, trying to rub the faint outline of her nipples against the fabric from my mind.

Be the good guy.

"How'd you sleep?" Better than me, I hope. But as I search for any hint of a shadow or bag under her eyes, a shitty part of me might be just a smidge bummed to see that she looks perfectly rested. Like she didn't lose a wink of sleep thinking about that moment in the bathroom last night.

"Great. In fact, I'm ready to run if you are," she says with a bounce and a smile. "We don't have anything scheduled for this morning, do we?"

Another ding to the ego. Sorry, buddy.

"Lunch with Walt and Janie at noon."

"Plenty of time then. I'll change first and meet you out front when you're ready."

Harlow

I HAD to get out of that room.

After tossing and turning half the night, staring at the ceiling, staring at the bathroom door, then staring at my phone when I realized staring was all I was going to be able to do—I couldn't take it another minute.

I'd just been creeping out of bed, hoping to change into my running gear and slink out before he woke up when the bed from Hell broadcast that Wade was awake. So my slinking plan was out the window and there wasn't any choice but to brave a visit to his side of the suite and see for myself whether there was anything weird lingering between us.

Newsflash: there wasn't. Not from his side anyway.

It was just Wade being Wade. No weighted pauses. No big, muscley hockey player prowling out of bed to back me into my room. Just a nice smile and a guy making plans for the day with his fake girlfriend.

Perfect.

Ten minutes later, he meets me on the grassy strip in front of the truck. And ten minutes after that, we're stretched and chatting as easily as we have all along.

It's another beautiful morning, and when we get out to the old Enderson water tower, instead of just running around it, Wade stops and gives me that too-tempting grin. "You afraid of heights?"

He cocks his head toward the tower, a dare gleaming in his eyes.

I love climbing. It's something I picked up imagining, like golf, skiing, and tennis, it would be as good a skill to have in business as my MBA. So far the only use I've had for it is my own enjoyment, but that's plenty.

"We're going up? Isn't that illegal?"

"Yep. And I wouldn't recommend it anywhere other than Enderson. But here... Well, it's the best view in town, and let's just say I've got one last free pass." Wade bites his bottom lip and then pulls a face. "But you can't tell anyone. For real. This is the *only* thing I do that breaks the rules. And my dad's buddy has been looking the other way since I was in high school. We have permission. So if you want to... we can."

I've never done anything like that before... I don't walk outside the lines. Ever. But for some reason, this man brings out a part of me that wants to grab hold of the adventure and just say yes.

"I'd love to."

A few minutes later, I'm rubbing my hands against my shorts as I sit over the treetops, rolling fields, and a handful of lakes with my feet dangling so high above the ground it feels like I'm flying.

"You weren't kidding. It's gorgeous up here."

"This is my favorite spot. Where I always came to think when I had a decision to make." Wade leans back on his arms with a peaceful smile. "Sometimes it was serious stuff, like how to handle hockey and football and what I wanted for my future. Sometimes it was about a girl."

My jaw drops. "Oh my God, Wade, is this a historic make-out point we're visiting? Is this where you brought your girls?"

He laughs as a breeze plays through his hair.

"Believe it or not, you're the first person I've ever brought up here."

That's not the answer I'm expecting, and a shiver tickles over my arms that has nothing to do with the moving air. "Why bring me?"

"You've given me this week back. And pretty sure I promised you some fun. Said I'd show you the best Enderson has to offer. Ask me? This is it."

"Well, thank you."

We stay there a while, talking about popcorn and people who mix candy into it, what to do on rainy days, and how he thinks I might be a secret jock. He's nuts and he's kind of wonderful. Then after we climb down, we walk back to the hotel, taking our time. No rush. No hurry. No emails or regulatory meetings. Just talking and laughing and me trying not to notice how different it feels to be with him than it's ever felt with a guy before.

Harlow

"I THOUGHT there was a rule about no touching?" Janie asks a few hours later, swirling a fry through her ketchup at our table in Sonny's Café. It seems like half the town stopped over to say hello to Wade when we first walked in... and even more to check in with Walt and Janie about the wedding.

She holds it up, and Walt leans over and takes it from her fingers with his mouth. They are ridiculously cute together.

"No touching *the girls*. The other way around though?" He winces at his brother. "Even, so, last night wasn't normal. Bro, I've never seen anything like that in my life."

Wade shrugs.

Walt turns to me with earnest eyes. "You should have seen this guy putting her off like a champ. Typical

Wade, trying to be polite. Doesn't want to be a dick or make a scene. Had to be a solid twenty minutes he kept setting this chick back from him with all the 'No, thank you's and 'Sorry, I have a girlfriend' business."

I bite my lip, imagining Wade trying to fight off yet another woman's unwanted advances. Then leaning into his side, I ask, "Sort of a running theme with you, huh?"

He lets out a low laugh, our secret hanging in that look between us. "Too bad you weren't there to help me out."

"Too bad."

And then he turns to his brother, who's watching us like he's never seen Wade flirt with a girl in his life. "No big deal. I mean, it all worked out in the end… Harlow helped me wash off all those hard-to-reach places."

The bounce of his eyebrows suggests he's talking about something more than me standing with him in the bathroom, and all I can do is laugh.

Janie rolls her eyes, giving her fiancé a shoulder bump. "Oh my God, with these two! Harlow, have you got siblings?"

"A brother, older by five years. Or half-brother. My dad's been married a few times. But between the age difference and rarely being in the same house, we're not close like these guys." Not to mention that we couldn't be less alike.

"That's too bad," Walt says, going after another fry. "He didn't get along with your mom?"

I take a sip of my iced tea, searching for an easy answer that won't invite more questions. But short of lying, there isn't one. "Actually, I don't know how they got along. My mother was killed in a car accident when I was an infant."

Wade reaches for my hand as Walt and Janie both tell me how sorry they are for my loss and I try to make them feel better about bringing it up.

"So you never knew your mother?" Janie asks, her eyes misty.

"Not really. I know things about her, of course. She was from Tamil Nadu in India and met my father while she was studying at the London School of Economics. They were married within months." And she was dead within a year.

I don't offer that last detail. It gives too much of the math away.

My father married my mother when she was pregnant with me.

I don't mention that I'm fairly confident he resented her for it. Or that it sometimes makes me sad to think about what that last year of her life might have been like living with a man who can't be bothered to hide his resentment for the people who inconvenience him. Or that what I just shared with them is the sum total of what I know about my mother.

Janie leaves her seat and, coming over beside mine, pulls me into a hug. It's so unexpected, so sweet and kind, I'm a little choked up when she pulls back.

"Did your dad marry again? Do you have a stepmom?" she asks, sliding back into her seat and beneath Walt's waiting arm.

"No. My mother was wife number three. And my father… Honestly, if it's not business, it doesn't really make his radar."

This is the kind of conversation I do anything to avoid. It's why I've always been a good listener and tend to ask more questions about others than I offer information about myself. I don't want to have to explain about the string of nannies who were as cool and detached as my father or why the only pictures of me from when I was a kid are the ones my teachers took at school.

I don't like feeling like the freak outcast, and the truth is, I can fake not being one with the best of them. Just so long as people don't ask me too many questions. Like how we celebrate holidays or what family vacations we've taken.

I take another long swallow of my tea and then throw a hand up like some exciting idea just came to me. "Hey, what's happening tonight? More wedding prep?"

Walt flags our server for the check and then flips Wade off when he tries to pick it up. "Everyone's heading over to the Den tonight. What do you say?"

Wade turns to me, brow raised in question. "What do you think, Good Girl? You up for some Enderson nightlife?"

I make a show of thinking it over. "I don't know, is this the kind of place where you'll be coming home with your shirt in tatters again?"

He gives me a grin-wink combo that's probably been setting panties on fire since the first time he stumbled on it. "Not unless you're the one tearing it off."

Chapter 11

Harlow

That afternoon, Wade takes me to the local bookstore—an *actual* store dedicated solely to *books*!—and we spend an hour and a half talking quietly within the narrow aisles about our favorite reads. Mine are all so outdated, I'm embarrassed. But Wade just nods, calling them classics and commenting on what he thought of one title or another himself.

He's a James Rollins fan, and when I admit I haven't read for pleasure in years, he buys me a paperback of my own. And as if that isn't enough to win Fake Boyfriend of the Century, then he takes me back to his parents' place where he hangs up the hammock so we can spend a couple hours reading together.

Grace brings us lemonade before she and Bill take off for something in the city. And Kelsey decides it's time to do some yard work and makes a big show of wrestling God-only-knows-what out of the shed.

And Wade… This guy is so completely unexpected.

So sweet.

So comfortable to rest my head on while I devour the first few chapters.

So adorable when he wants to know where I am in the story and how I like it.

So confusing, because he's so completely different from the men I usually date… But every time he gives me that smile that lasts a little longer than I expect it to, the butterflies start up in my belly and I wonder what it would be like, if just for this one week, I could be different too.

Later, when we're back at the hotel getting ready to hit the Den, Walt texts, begging off for the bar because Janie's cousin needed an emergency sitter.

"Do they need any help?" I ask, fastening my gold hoop earring.

"Nah, they're good," Wade says from his side of the wall. "Just can't make it tonight. What do you think, we could stay in and—"

I turn to where Wade's standing in the archway between our rooms. He's dressed in a pair of faded jeans and a black shirt that's open at the top and has to be made-to-measure the way it fits around his biceps, chest, and shoulders without hanging like a sail around his abs.

He looks really good.

And he was saying something.

"Sorry, what?"

He opens his mouth, but nothing comes out. His eyes rake over me from top to bottom before scanning the space around the suite with a frown.

I shouldn't have put on the heavier eye makeup, but Janie mentioned dressing up for the night out. "Wade?"

I don't want him to think I'm a Kelsey. That I'm trying to push for something—

"Let's get out of here," Wade says, shoving his hands in his pockets and taking a step back. "The bar will be great."

God, he doesn't even look at me.

"You sure you're up for going out with it just being the two of us?" I ask, feeling unsure. It's not like I can take the makeup off without it being weird.

Wade grabs his keys. "This is Enderson. Trust me, it's never just the two of us."

THE DEN IS A WARM, relaxed space with an open-cabin kind of feel. Everything is made of heavy logs, blond and high gloss. There are high-top tables with tall stools surrounding a bar built from more of the same, and as we push through the heavy door, Wade tells me the owner made almost all of it by hand.

I can't even imagine having the time or passion for such an undertaking, but the result is gorgeous.

"Damn, baby, get that sweet ass over here!"

Wade laughs, ducking his head at the gravelly voice bellowing across the room. His eyes cut to mine, and he winces. "That's Tommy. And, don't take it personally, but he's talking to me."

I don't even have a chance to ask before Wade's towing me across the bar to an oversized booth built into the corner.

Two of the guys climb out and are smacking Wade's back, exchanging manly handclaps, while the third sits deep in the booth, watching with a smirk. Wade introduces the first two as Tommy and DJ and then, almost as an unpleasant afterthought, the guy in back as Collin.

Wade signals for a couple more glasses and another pitcher, which land on the table in a matter of seconds. But before we can sit, more friends from high school are coming over. More guys who went to high school with his dad and even a guy whose lawn Wade used to mow stops by.

He tries to introduce me, but everyone's talking over each other, giving him a hard time about how long it's been since he was home. Asking about his mom. Talking about some kid they think is going to take them to State.

That part sounds familiar. The arm. The snap. The—

"Yo, Wade's girl," the guy from the back of the booth—Collin—says, leaning across the curved bench with a beckoning wave. "The prodigal son's return always takes a while. Have a beer and take a load off."

It seems like a better plan than standing awkwardly beside my fake boyfriend while half his graduating class closes in on him. But before I can let go of Wade's hand, his grip on mine firms and I'm tucked back to his side. Those laughing blue eyes turn hard as they meet Collin's.

And that is not something I've seen from Wade before. Well, maybe close to the one he gave O'Dwyer back at the Five Hole after I humiliated myself in front of him that first day.

"Take it easy, man." Collin starts climbing out of the booth, grabbing his glass on the way. "*Joking.* And I'm taking off anyway."

Wade's jaw is set hard, the muscle jumping, once,

twice, as Collin claps the other guys on the shoulders and then, cutting through the crowd, heads for the exit.

I start to ask, but he shakes his head. "That guy's trouble. I'll tell you later."

There's an awkward beat, but Tommy clears his throat and wedges his barrel chest past me to slide into the booth himself. Patting the bench beside him, he gives me a wide grin. "Come on, Harlow. Tell me how this guy fast-talked you into a trip to exotic Enderson?"

Wade

I AM NOT a good fucking guy.

Tommy and DJ have been telling Harlow stories about the misadventures of my youth for the last hour, giving her crap about never having watched a football game, giving me crap about how they totally get why she hasn't seen a hockey game either, and making the girl who isn't actually mine laugh like... Damn, like *I like* making her laugh.

And I'm jealous.

Which is crazy because I'm not the jealous type, and it's bullshit because I'm not supposed to want this to be real. We have a deal. And I don't want to be the guy flipping the script.

That's why I had to get her the hell out of that hotel room tonight.

One look at Harlow with those smokey eyes and her hair pinned back so I could see the silky length of her neck on one side—damn—I knew we had to get out. That if we didn't, I'd end up putting some move on her and being the total douche I'm trying so hard not to be.

One week. That's all I've got to make it. And then once we get past the *I Do*s, once I have her back in Chicago where she's got home-ice advantage—then I'll pull out everything I've got.

Probably on her doorstep.

But not now. Not here. Not when I can't fucking tell if the signals I'm getting off her are about perfecting our *fake*, or because she's feeling it too.

Harlow turns in her seat, eyes bright and beautiful, still laughing from whatever story Tommy was telling her. "Wade, you were such a hellion! And here I'd been so sure I was signing on with a *good guy*."

I want to be. But even her teasing me with my own words is working against that effort, doing things to me it shouldn't.

Climbing out of the booth, I hold out my hand, and when she gives me hers, I draw her along with me.

"Are we leaving?"

"No way, Good Girl. We're dancing."

Her eyes go wide but I don't give her a chance to

say no before I'm pulling her in against me and spinning her around. And the quick move pays off, because then she's laughing, her hands against my chest, holding tight to my shirt as she finds her balance.

God, that's nice.

"Wade! I'm not— I don't really—"

"Sure you do." Keeping an arm behind her, I lead us onto the small dance floor that's been filling up since we arrived.

"So we're selling it now?" she asks, hands sliding up to my shoulders. "Anyone in particular you're trying to convince, or just Enderson as a whole?"

Pretty sure I'm selling it to all the guys who keep staring at her, wondering whether they've got a shot at the prettiest girl here.

They don't.

"Sorry about that business with Collin, back there. I wasn't expecting to see him—though I probably should have."

"Not your favorite person?"

"Not even close." More than ten years later, and I still can't think about the guy without feeling like I'm suffocating beneath the weight of his bad choices. "Tommy and DJ say he's turned it around since high school, but back then? He was the kind of fuckup that could drag you down in a blink."

Her eyes go wide. "Did something happen with you?"

"Yeah. I didn't know it at the time, but he was into some pretty bad shit. And just being near him almost cost me my future."

She stops moving. "Oh my God, Wade."

Aww hell, I shouldn't have brought it up. I'll tell her the whole story sometime. But not on a night I promised to show her a good time.

"Hey, don't worry." I pull her back into motion, holding her a little closer. Giving her the smile she always gives back. "It all got straightened out in the end. But if you want to know why I'm so serious about keeping my nose clean… that guy is it."

She pats my chest. "You're a good guy."

"Don't forget it, Good Girl."

We talk and dance. Harlow moves with me, her soft curves driving me out of my mind, her laugh making me ache for more. The next song has a heavier beat, a rhythm we fall into too easily. Our bodies sync up, the space between us becoming nonexistent.

She's got one hand at the back of my neck. My arm is wrapped around her with my hand on the far side of her waist.

I'm not breaking the rules.

It's just dancing.

It's for show.

Harlow's eyes lift to meet mine. Hold there. Her fingers move through my hair. Mine tighten at the side of her dress.

What if I'm not reading this wrong? What if—

A throat clears.

It's fucking Tommy standing beside us, his shit-eating grin begging for a fist, hands pressed together into a wedge he's literally driving between us.

"Enough of that," he sort of sings with that chainsaw voice, prying us apart. "Wade, don't be a dick, and stop hogging the girl."

Dude.

He ignores the threat in my eyes, hip-checking me out of the way to grab Harlow's hand. And as if cutting in on my girl wasn't bad enough, the fucker spins her out and then reels her back into his arms in a showy move that makes mine look like crap.

Jesus, I can feel the caveman thumping on my chest.

Okay, maybe I owe Tommy something other than a good beating because that was close.

I head to an open spot at the bar where Carol pushes a water my way.

Delighted, Harlow waves to me from over Tommy's shoulder. Her face is pure joy, and it's a hell of a lot safer that I'm seeing it from across the room.

What if she lets me kiss her and things get weird? We're sharing a hotel room. For another week. The only place she'd have to go is home, and I don't want it to go that way. I don't want to lose her.

It's fine. Nothing happened.

I lean back against the bar, watching Harlow get danced around the Den by my oldest buddy. He dips her, chuckling, while I shore up my friend zone. I remind myself of all the reasons it's the safest place for us, when reason number one walks through the door.

Kelsey. And she's already seen me.

Shit.

There's no pretending I don't see her. No ignoring the fact that she's already coming this way. Maybe if I just brush past her with a quick hello and head to the back like I'm going to take a leak, I can dodge another talk.

I push off my stool, but before I take a single step, there's a warm, soft, and slightly sweaty woman bounding into my arms—*Harlow*—and I drop back down with a smile.

"Hey there, Good Girl."

"Miss me, handsome?" she asks with a glint in her eyes that says she saw exactly what was happening.

"Absolutely. But a reunion like this makes it all worthwhile."

She tosses her head back with a laugh, letting all those rebel ribbons of dark silk shake out. *Damn.* And when she comes up again, the look in her eyes is—I swallow hard—it's really fucking convincing. Almost as convincing as the slow, hip-winding dance she's doing in the vee of my legs.

Down boy. It's for show.

Her hand snakes up my chest, her fingers walking over the buttons until she reaches the second from the top and one hooks inside. Eyes locked with mine, she bites her bottom lip and draws me in. Closer, closer. So close, I'm hovering a breath above her, my arm supporting her as she bows back.

"Wade," she murmurs. "If you want to make a point, now seems like a really good time to do it."

I shouldn't. I know better. But— "You want to pull the pin on this grenade?"

She nods, one brow arched. "Think you can handle it?"

This girl.

Holding her steady with the arm at her back, I slide my free hand around her neck and take the kiss she's offering with the barest brush of my mouth over hers. A slow pull and draw against lips that give and part, welcoming that one taste I know I shouldn't have.

Fuck, she's sweet.

Sweet and warm and pressing closer, opening wider, linking her arms tighter.

I don't want to think about the fact that Harlow likes to win. That she gets off on blowing the bell curve.

Or that she has an almost compulsive need to follow through on her goals.

All I want is the taste of her mouth, the catch of her breath, and that silky moan begging me to sink deeper, to take more. To haul her against my body and—

Fuck!

Dragging myself back, I shake my head. *"Harlow."*

My heart's pounding, my body fighting my mind.

Our eyes lock. It's only for a second, but Christ, it's enough. I want to pull her back into my arms. Find a dark corner and tell her I don't give a fuck about Kelsey. The only thing that matters is her.

Instead, "We have to stop."

"Really? Kissing you is pretty fun." She's breathless. Those midnight eyes trailing after my mouth. "Maybe we shouldn't stop just yet."

I groan, liking the sound of that way too much. "It's better than fun. But if I kiss you again"—I run my hand over the length of her hair, barely resisting the urge to bury my fingers in it—"it won't be about Kelsey. It won't be pretend or just for show."

Harlow stills. "It won't?"

"Hell, no, it won't. I'm trying to be the good guy I promised you I was." I shake my head. "The truth is, I want *you*. And if you want to keep things the way they are or be done with them altogether, then that's what we'll do. But if you want me to kiss you again—and make no mistake, I want to—then it's going to be real."

She wets her bottom lip, meeting my eyes. "You *are* a good guy. And I appreciate the respect you've been showing me." Fingers trailing down my shirt, she leans in again, letting her lips brush the corner of my mouth. "But what if I don't want to do the right thing or make the sensible choice? What if I know exactly what this is… and what it isn't? And, just this once, I want to have some fun with you?"

"Just this once?"

She nods, taking an emboldened step into my space, so once again I have that mind-blowing press of her body against mine.

"Just tonight. No expectations. No consequences."

Damn it. That's what I thought she meant. And I can't be surprised. I'm not her type and her life hasn't changed… But then neither have I.

I'm still the guy in college who didn't make sense. The off fit. The guy on the bench who talked his way into one shift in the game. Who knew what was at stake and wouldn't stop until one shift became one period. One start. One score after another. One tryout. One trip up to the big show because one too many regular players were hurt.

I'm the guy who doesn't fuck up when he gets a shot.

And that's what this is.

"Wade, kiss me again."

Bypassing the lips I want to sink into with everything I have, I bring my mouth to her ear.

"If tonight's all I get"—and I'm going to make damn sure it won't be—"no way am I sharing even one more minute with Kelsey or anyone else here. Time to go, Harlow."

Chapter 12

Harlow

Wade takes my hand and the bar falls away.

Just this once.

The words run through my mind on repeat, shocking me more each time. I'm so out of my depth I can barely breathe. Can barely think of anything but the firm grasp of his hand around mine and the tiny electric charges tingling up my arm from it.

The cool night air teases my skin as we cross the lot, gravel shifting beneath our feet. Our eyes meet. Our pace quickens. By the time we reach the truck at the back, I'm shaking.

There's a single weighted beat, so heavy it almost

hurts, and then we collide in an urgent crush. The sounds of need and relief meeting on our tongues.

He pins me against the passenger door, kissing me hard.

God, he's so big.

"Been telling myself to leave you alone," he growls against my neck. "Been killing me."

His mouth is everywhere, his hands the same. And I'm drunk on his kiss, drowning in it. There's nothing but him and me and this burning need for *more*.

I can't get enough.

Pressure coils tight in my center and my breasts ache for his touch. It's never been like this. I've never *wanted* like this.

"Wade," I gasp, my fingers burrowing deeper into his hair, pulling him closer, begging with my mouth and body for more. More of his tongue. More of his hands. More of that rough, masculine sound rumbling up from deep in his chest when my hips shift against his. Please, more of that.

"Need to touch you." His hand's beneath my skirt, fingers slipping higher.

Yes. "Touch me."

"Feel how wet you are."

My breath catches and my body quakes.

God, that mouth. So much wetter now.

No one, no one in my life has ever spoken to me like

that. And if someone had asked me yesterday if I thought I'd like it, I would have told them no.

But the clenching twist deep inside, wringing liquid heat between my legs, tells me that would have been a lie.

I want to hear more. But I don't know what to say. So instead, I speak with my body. My hand reaching for his, guiding it that last inch toward contact.

"Fuck, that's hot." Eyes locked with mine, he drags the pads of his fingers over my panties. *"Soaked."*

This is crazy. Reckless.

Incredible.

Heart racing, body thrumming, I try to check over my shoulder. Make sure we're still alone. But the truck behind me blocks the view.

There's no way for me to know if someone's coming. We should stop, we should—

Whoa. "That's— That's—" My breath catches as Wade rubs another slow circle around my clit. "So good."

"Trust me, Good Girl?" he asks, circling again and then petting me with the full length of those thick, long fingers. Teasing me. Making me clench and ache.

"I do." Maybe it's crazy, but it's true.

"I said I wasn't sharing you." His eyes flick from mine to the bar in the distance. "No one can see."

Thank God, because I don't want him to stop. I

don't want to think. I just want to stay in this moment with Wade driving me wild, the pleasure usually so hard to chase rushing closer with every second that passes.

And then he's kissing me again, his tongue thrusting hard and deep as he teases beneath the silk of my panties. His rough fingers so good I gasp.

"You like that?" he murmurs against my lips. "Want more?"

"Yes." I'm close, nodding desperately now.

Wade strokes through my slickness again, then, eyes locked with mine, he presses inside.

My eyes go wide, my breath catching on a fractured cry he cuts off with his kiss.

He works in and out, slow and steady. One finger becomes two as he dirty-talks against my lips. *"So fucking good… so wet for me… feel you squeezing me…"*

It's never been like this.

"So tight…"

He's stroking deeper, stretching me more.

"So sweet… making me crazy…"

Oh God. *"Wade."*

His thumb presses firm. "Come for me, Good Girl…"

And that does it.

I'm done. Crying out into his mouth as the pleasure surges and breaks, crashing hard through my center again and again until I'm limp and breathless, clinging to the man who just changed my world.

Our eyes meet and I catch my breath enough to speak. "You are crazy fun."

He laughs, pulling me into his chest as he opens my door. "In the truck, Harlow. I'm not done with you yet."

Wade

THE DRIVE to the hotel is torture.

But getting back to our room and getting Harlow beneath me is mission-critical, so I keep my hands on the wheel and my eyes on the road. And when she leans across the front and slides her hand up my thigh, I tell her that unless she wants me to pull over and fuck her against the steering wheel right here on Main Street, she's gotta stop.

She doesn't. And she makes a liar out of me too because as bad as I want to hear her coming apart for me again, I've maxed out my risk-taking today.

That business in the parking lot? Not my usual MO, but damn, I couldn't stop. Not when we had the woods behind us and the truck blocking the view of anyone coming out of the bar. Not when she was giving me those sexy, needy sounds and pulling my hand between her legs.

The last half mile is brutal, but somehow, I make it to the hotel, park, and get Harlow out of the truck without seeing how hard or how fast I can get her to come on my hand again. Somehow we get past the front desk and out of the elevator without getting arrested. But once the doors open on our floor, it's on.

I'm backing her down the hallway, mouth fused to hers. She's already got half the buttons of my shirt open. When she misses a step, I catch her, lifting her against me.

Her back meets the wall between rooms 303 and 305, her legs coming up around my waist as I rock into her heat. Two doors down, it's my back at the plaster, her hands fumbling with my belt. Finally, we make it and stumble into the room, propelled by some hard-driving insanity.

"Clothes," she gasps. *"Hurry."*

I nod, grabbing the back of my shirt and whipping it over my head. "Need to get inside of you."

Only she stops. Eyes wide and staring at my chest, she swallows.

And then instead of stripping off her sexy dress, she steps back into my space and presses her hands flat against my abs and smooths them up over my pecs.

My ego lifts his head, fucking sighs in relief.

Five seconds ago, I was completely on board with the hurry, hurry. But having Harlow's hands on my bare skin for the first time makes me want to slow down.

"It's crazy," she murmurs, tracing my shoulders with her fingertips. "We've been all over each other for the last couple of days. Faking like we've been together this way. But it's all new."

"It is." And not just that I'm finally able to run my thumb across the lush swell of her bottom lip. It's that this *feeling* I have when I'm with her is *new*.

I've had girlfriends.

I've gotten caught up in women.

But *this*? This is different.

I want to tell her she's special, drop the words like kisses across her body, let her see it in my eyes. But that's not what tonight's about. Until I convince her otherwise, tonight is about *tonight*.

Still trailing her fingertips across my skin, she brings her lips into the mix. The light scrape of her teeth. The smallest taste from her tongue.

"Harlow."

She hums, sliding her arms around me and moving on to a slow, openmouthed exploration that's so sweet and sexy, I have to clasp my hands behind my head to keep from grabbing her and tossing her onto the bed.

"You're killing me with that mouth."

Another soft hum. "Your body's making me do it."

Her kisses drift lower, and while I love the direction of her thoughts, it's not what I want tonight.

"Come here," I say, bringing her up. I gather the dress I've already taken more than my share of liberties with and draw it over her head, leaving her in a pale pink bra and matching panty set that's fucking gorgeous against the darker hues of her skin.

"Beautiful." For a guy who likes to use his mouth, it's all I've got.

"You make me feel that way. You make me—" She shakes her head, looking at me with a mixture of heat and wonder that has me pulling her in for another kiss.

When I have her mouth beneath mine again, her soft moans slipping over my tongue, I wrap my arms around her and carry her to the bed.

I lay her down, pressing the condom from my wallet into her hand as I taste the spot beneath her jaw and skim the line of her collarbone with my nose. Nuzzling lower, I tease the swell of her breasts while easing the straps of her bra from one shoulder and then the other.

She reaches behind her for the clasp and then those silky cups fall away, freeing the full mounds.

So sexy.

I draw one tight, beaded nipple into my mouth, sucking and flicking until she's arching beneath me, her knees sliding restlessly against my jeans.

"Naked," she pants, making me grin when she starts working them down with her feet.

"Naked," I agree, catching her panties as I back off the bed. And damn, the needy sound she makes when my cock springs free is about the hottest fucking thing I've ever heard.

Taking it in hand, I give myself a slow stroke to torture us both. Her mouth drops open and yeah, that does it. I'm back on the bed, crawling up her body. Groaning when she rises up, reaching for my kiss.

Our tongues glide together, wet and hot. Urgent.

I rock between her spread legs, coating my shaft with her need. Teasing her clit with the ridge of my cock and then dragging it back and forth through her folds until we're slick, groaning, treading dangerously close to the line I never cross.

I won't. I won't.

Fuck—

I break away for the condom and then she's pulling me back to her. Sucking on my tongue and moaning around mine. I press her knee up and open. Line up, so I'm right there. So close, I can feel the needy pulse of her body begging to take mine.

But I want the words.

"Tell me, Good Girl."

Her breath is ragged, desperate. "*Please.*"

Please.

She's killing me.

I push into her slippery, wet heat, clenching my jaw as she squeezes and hugs me. Pulls me deeper and gasps when she's taken me as far as she can. Our eyes meet and hold, while I wait for her to adjust.

Another clingy grasp, and I start to move, slowly. Pulling back through that wet velvet grip, back, back, and then sliding in again, deep, deeper. She takes more of me this time, clenching around me when I bottom out.

And then we're moving in time, straining together.

We're all rolling hips and grasping hands, deep kisses, sweat-slicked limbs.

"You like that, Good Girl?" I ask, grinding deep and using my hips to stir inside her.

She nods, quick and desperate, her fingers gripping my shoulder and arm.

"You want more?" Shifting my weight to get a different angle, I give her a few shallow thrusts that hit another sweet spot. Watch as her mouth opens and closes in a silent plea.

She's almost there.

"You want my cock so deep inside that sweet pussy you'll feel me for days?"

The hard pulse of her body around mine gives me the answer even before she shudders out, "*Y-yes.*"

Getting closer.

I tease us both through another short thrust and then I give it to her.

Full length. Hard and deep. Burying myself so far inside I meet her throbbing little clit with my groin… and she comes apart for me, crying my name as her body grips mine like a fist, pulling me over the edge with her.

When we can breathe again, she turns to where I'm collapsed at her side. "You've got skills, Wade Grady."

I grin, wiping my brow on the back of my arm. "You haven't seen half of them yet."

Chapter 13

Harlow

I wake to a low masculine growl that sounds like satisfaction and contentment all in one. Wade pulls me into his body, his breath warm and soft against my shoulder when everything else about him is spectacularly hard.

"You awake, Good Girl?"

"I am." I smile, turning over in his arms so we're facing one another. It's morning and our one night is done. Still, I'm not quite ready to give up the connection and intimacy, and I snuggle closer. "We're late for our run."

Wade rolls his head back and forth against his pillow in what I'm taking to mean no. "Not leaving this bed until you kick me out."

"That so?" Trailing my fingers over his shoulders and chest, I soak in the feel of him. A few more minutes won't hurt anyone.

He catches my hand with his and holds it against his heart. It's such a tender move. So sweet. So Wade. And for a minute I imagine being able to wake up like this together each morning.

It would never work, but it's a nice thought. The kind vacations are made of.

"You okay about last night?" he asks, eyes holding steady with mine.

So much more than okay. "Last night was amazing. I usually don't…" I can't believe I'm considering even telling him this, but as evidenced by my actions last night, I trust him with things I'd never trust anyone else with. "Okay, I've never actually—when I'm alone I have, but even then—"

In my mind, it was so much easier to say the words. But trying to voice them, I can feel the heat burning through my cheeks.

Oh my God, why did I think I could tell him?

I start to turn away, but he catches my shoulder and gently guides me back so he's leaning above me, those gorgeous blue eyes peering down into mine.

"Are you saying I'm the first guy who's ever made you come?"

"I've only been with a few men, and no one serious.

But it's never been like that." Never like my next breath depended on having just that much more of him. With the others, it had been more about waiting it out for them to finish.

Wade slowly shakes his head.

"Good Girl, what kind of guys are you dating?"

The wrong kind. "The kind who are probably more interested in my father than they are in me." Another admission I can't believe I'm making.

"Wait, what? Why?" Then, "I'm starting to think I'm failing at this fake boyfriend thing… Who's your dad, anyway?"

And that, right there, is what makes Wade so perfect for this break out of time.

"He's got some clout in the financial world. A lot of connections. And to be honest, most of the men I've dated swim in the same circles."

He nods, seeming to process this information. Then he squints. "You keep telling me I'm not your type. You don't dig jocks. And yet, not one of these *suits* who supposedly *are* your type has gotten you—"

My hand covers his mouth, holding back those last words as I shush him with a laugh. "Okay, fine. I would like to amend my previous statement. It's possible that I might be marginally attracted to men like you."

Wade's brow rises and he shifts over me, sliding his knee between mine.

"Marginally?" His eyes drop to my mouth as he brings his thigh against me. "And for a minute there, I thought my ego had a chance. But you're just downright trying to kill the poor guy, aren't you?"

My answering laugh is breathless and a bit broken. And then my hands are on his chest, sliding up over his shoulders and neck, my fingers sifting their way back into his hair.

This isn't the plan.

I was going for a swift exit, intending to make the transition back to *friendly* and *fake* as easy as possible.

I could stop this. All it would take is one word. Probably less than that if I meant it… But the hard-muscled friction he's giving me feels so good.

"I thought last night was a one-time thing?"

He lowers his mouth to my ear, catching the lobe between his teeth for a gentle tug. "Last night was a three-time thing if I'm remembering correctly." He shifts lower, his tongue working over the tender skin beneath. "But maybe you need one more?"

I bow into his touch, leaning into that sensual space Wade carved out for me.

His lips ghost over mine, barely making contact. "Or I can stop if you want."

He pulls back, showing me the hunger in his eyes, the taunting gleam that says he knows I want him as much as he wants me.

"Say it, Good Girl."

My knees slide up to his hips, my heels pressing at the backs of his thighs. "Don't stop."

Wade

I DON'T STOP. Not until I've made up for a few of the shortcomings from Harlow's dating past. Knowing that not one of those worthless dickheads was able to satisfy her is the mouth-to-mouth resuscitation my ego has been waiting for. But damn, I hate that that's how it's been for her.

So yeah, I make it last. I make it good.

I even make her beg just a little on this last one. But judging by how hard she comes around me and the following assault of kisses raining over my face, neck, and shoulders, I'm gonna go out on a limb and say she doesn't mind.

Thing is, it's just sex. Pretty spectacular sex, yeah, but as much as I'm hoping Harlow has had a miraculous change of heart on the "just" subject… I'm not banking on it.

Turning on my side, I trace light patterns around the flat of her belly.

"So was that *just these four times…* or do we want to

go with *six*?"

She laughs, and it's this breathless sated sound so sweet I'm pretty sure I'll do anything to hear it again.

"What? I don't know how you're counting."

"For real? You're counting?" she asks, eyes soft, lips kiss-swollen and tipped up at one side.

My chin pulls back. "*You're not?* How do you grade if you aren't keeping score?"

Lifting her hand a couple inches, she gives it a limp wave. "You blew the curve."

That's right, I did. But this is *Harlow*. "Good Girl, are you seriously telling me that you'd accept that generic result? That you wouldn't demand accuracy in reporting?"

She bites her lip, that hot-as-hell light firing up in her eyes. "You're right. I would."

So sexy.

I growl, reaching for her again, but she flees the bed with a shriek, pulling half the covers with her. "Fine, it was a six-time thing. *Six*. But there's no seven. This was it, okay, Wade?"

I flash a wink. "Got it."

Chapter 14

Wade

This is *not* it.

Harlow escapes to the shower, and I jam my legs into a pair of jeans and a hoody and cut out of the room. I need a consult, and there's only one place in the whole of Enderson and outlying where I can be sure it won't be overheard.

Two minutes later I'm slamming the door to the truck, Axel's voice coming through the sound system.

"Dude, Nettie says this girl is good people, so if you're calling in some panic because your fake girlfriend turned out to be psycho—the problem is you."

I drop an f-bomb and knock my head back against the rest. "This is how you answer the phone? What if I'm calling on speaker from my mom's kitchen?"

"Are you?" His voice is one hundred percent no-shits-to-give.

"No." What a dick.

"Did you spend the last fifteen hours freeing one limb from the duct tape holding you to a urine-soaked bed?"

"No." But that visual's not going anywhere anytime soon.

"Suspect she's after your kidney?"

"Axe," I growl, only to hear the asshole chuckle across the line.

"So spit it out. What's the problem?"

"I want her."

"She's hot. But don't be a dumbass. You got a week left and you don't want this chick catching feelings… so keep her away from your favorite stick."

"That's the thing—"

"Dude. She already got it?" A string of muttered cursing flows through the truck. "Haven't you ever heard of jerking off? For fuck's sake, man. I was kidding about the duct tape and kidney thing. But now—who fucking knows? Nettie is going to be so pissed. Have you ever seen her mad?"

I blink. His married banker? "Have you?"

I hear a muffled grunt and what I'm guessing is the sound of my teammate propping himself up in bed. "Not really."

"Axe, you're missing the point. I *want* her to catch feelings."

"Huh, not following."

"I don't know what it is about her. Yeah, she's gorgeous and smart and sexy. But it's more than that. When I talk to her—hell, about anything—it just clicks. Like she gets what I'm saying, and I can't wait to hear what she thinks. Axe, this girl makes me laugh."

He grunts the grunt of the unimpressed. "Everybody makes you laugh."

"No. Not like this." Not where I feel it deep in my chest. "It's different with her, man. It's like I want to stay up all fucking night to see how much I can find out."

"She know how bad you got it for her?"

I stare out over the dash, see Sunday-morning Enderson coming to life. "Nah. I don't think so. I mean, we spent the night together, but… she's not like the other girls."

He huffs out one of those chill laughs. "Not chasing your ass, you mean?"

"Not even fucking close." I stack my arms over the wheel. "You know what she told me? I'm not her type. She's not into jocks, which is pretty fucking funny considering she's sort of one herself and just doesn't realize it."

"Hmm, so you're good enough for one night, but you can't talk this chick into an actual date?"

Glaring at the speaker, I can practically see his shoulders shaking. "Fuck off. This isn't funny."

"The way you're always talking people into stupid shit they don't want to do, it kind of is."

I'm about to hang up, but then he comes back. "So there's chemistry, yeah? You're not the kind of guy she goes for... but she did. Describe it."

"Axe, you can fuck right off."

"Dude, not her 'O' face. Jesus. I'm asking if this was one of those 'fuck it, why not' moments. Or was she serving up those looks? You know the ones. They're all about more and deeper, but in the *feelings*, not *feelin' it*, way."

"Yeah, I know the looks. But there's a problem. She's faking being my girlfriend. My sexy, long-term, serious girlfriend. And she's super intense about getting shit right. So yeah, she's nailed the looks. But—" I think about that moment in the bathroom after the bachelor party, and when I'd been holding her in my arms on the dance floor—before fucking Tommy broke it up. "Hell, there are times when it's just us, when we're talking and it's like she's seeing something she didn't expect. But I don't think I fit in with her plans."

"Uh-huh... We'll call that a solid maybe."

I blow a breath out my nose. Why did I call this guy

again? The closest he's come to commitment is buying the building half the team lives in. "Forget it."

"Right. Not sure you're capable of forgetting anything you care about, but whatever."

"Axe."

That fucker yawns. "Chill. I've got a plan."

I sit back. "Yeah?"

This is the reason I called him. For all the shit he gives, Axe has been known to offer some pretty solid advice.

"You're gonna have to think like a bunny."

I cough. "What the fuck does that mean?"

This guy is going into the boards *so hard* next time we hit the ice.

"It means, you gotta work your *assets*, dipshit. Be casual, like you dig what's going on between you, but if it's over thirty seconds from now, you're walking away smiling. No moony-eyed confessions about how she feeds your soul or any of that bullshit. Give her what she wants—and the fact that you're calling me tells me whatever went down last night was good enough that she's going to want more. So be *easy*. No threat. Just another pro-hockey player with all the fixin's, available if she's into it. And then when she is… make it count. Make it so good, she has to think long and fucking hard about what her type is, after all." A deep, satisfied breath sounds through the line. "Be the bunny, dude."

Harlow

I'M NOT sure what to expect when I get out of the shower, but Wade picking up the suite, muttering something about his teammate being an epic asshole, isn't it. He doesn't elaborate, instead asking if I'm feeling more pancakes or omelets, teasing me about my runner's guilt, and then hopping in the shower himself.

No weird vibes. No awkward tension.

It's nice. Normal.

Okay, yes, maybe I'm aware of Wade on a level I wasn't before.

And maybe I'm thinking about the things we did and how incredibly good he was at doing them. Yes.

But that's to be expected.

It would be *more* weird if I didn't, especially since the man took me to places no man has taken me before.

So… a weirdly normal start to a day I was worried might be just plain weird.

We have pancakes at this cute place in the next town over. Wade is all grins, some wolfish flirting, and as easygoing as a girl aiming for a single night of fun could ask for.

Sure, every so often, I need a minute to shake off a

memory so carnal, so *visceral* I can still practically feel him inside of me. But again… to be expected.

Last night didn't change anything other than to restore the ego he's always accusing me of trying to take out.

We spend most of the afternoon and evening helping Walt and Janie move into the house they won't be living in until they get back from their honeymoon. After, we eat pizza on the floor in the empty space where the dining room set will go and play Monopoly surrounded by boxes in the living room. With the limited audience, there's a minimum of showy relationship stuff, but the frequent contact that's become almost second nature between us remains.

The laughter still comes as easily as the conversation. And those glancing check-ins still feel as uncomplicated and reassuring as they have since Wade picked me up that first afternoon. Maybe more.

For a woman who's never really had the opportunity for casual sex, I'm kind of feeling like I nailed this thing.

Yes, yes, maybe I find my eyes on him a bit more often. But now *I know* what's under those clothes, and it's impressive.

Which is a completely reasonable, normal, and objective observation.

I totally nailed this thing.

That's what I'm thinking as we pull into the hotel. It's after ten and the stars are out. The lot's as empty as it was when we got in last night. We walk up to the front, but I can still hear the echoes of our breathless laughter and feel the urgency and pull of all that *hurry, faster, please* lingering in the air around us.

Wade chats in the elevator, his arm thrown around me in a casual hold. No big deal.

So why are there three hundred butterflies batting around my belly?

The doors slide open at our floor. The hall is empty, silent. No trace of our stumbling desperation from the night before. But I can feel the achy twist inside and phantom press of his body against mine as we pass the wall between 303 and 305.

Inside our room, Wade closes the door behind us and pulls me in for a hug, thanking me for helping out today. Some distant part of my brain registers that if I hadn't been there, Kelsey would have. That there's a reason I'm in this hotel with him…

I try to concentrate, except Wade's arms are still around me, leaving me awash in the clean masculine scent of the man who spent the majority of last night making me moan.

God, he smells so good. I want to bury my face in his chest, strip off his shirt and—

His arms tighten, pulling me that much closer.

It's so good.

It's *too* good, setting off a slow churn deep in my center. The awareness I've been dismissing all day runs hot like an electric charge beneath my skin, shorting out everything beyond *hurry, faster, please.*

He's still talking. "… don't see my brother enough, and to be able to sit and hear about his plans. Get a glimpse of the life ahead of him. It means a lot to me."

Right. I take a shallow breath.

He loosens and pulls back. "You okay?"

Dodging the eye contact, I force a laugh. Wave a hand. "Totally. Yes. Fine."

His eyes narrow and I can feel him studying me.

I will *not* make this weird.

Which means I won't think about the bed being less than ten feet away or how our bodies are making more contact than not. *Gah.*

That stitch between his eyes smooths and he steps back.

Never have I been so grateful for a single foot of space.

I take a deep breath. Let it out, still reeling from my reaction to being this close to the scene of the crime. I didn't expect it to affect me this way.

"Well, I'm glad it was a good day." I'm glad it was normal and not weird, and that Wade seems as comfortable putting our one night behind us as I am.

"Considering how it started, I'm going with this being a *great* day." Wade reaches over his shoulder and grabs a fistful of his shirt, yanking it overhead.

I think I make a noise that's not totally unaffected, but thankfully, he doesn't notice. He wads the shirt into a ball and tosses it into the other room. "I'd even go so far as to say it was a phenomenal day if it ended the way it began."

"Wha—"

He cuts me off with a quick kiss at my temple and another too-potent hit of concentrated *sexy*. "But I respect that you aren't interested. So we're sticking with a solid *great*."

This time I don't even know what I say.

"I'm going to grab a quick shower." Unbuckling his belt, he heads back.

Which is normal too, I think.

Then stopping at the door, he turns and props his forearm against the frame in a pose so potently masculine I lose my breath. How can anyone be that hot? Absently, he rubs his free hand over the packed muscles of his chest and down the hills and valleys of his abdomen before hooking his thumb in the already dangerously low waist of his shorts.

I open my mouth.

Hear the click of my throat.

Close it.

"Tomorrow, we're going to Janie's parents' in the afternoon. You'll like it. Nice place on Big Lake. We used to swim there when we were kids… I think Walt's got a few more guys coming into town…"

I nod, not quite sure what he said. Stare as he pushes off the doorframe, the movement highlighting the flex and give of too many muscles at once.

He turns on the shower, sticking his hand under the spray before grabbing a towel from the rack.

It's not weird that he hasn't closed the door yet.

"…but if it's too long of a day, I can pick you up later." He swings the door closed about three-quarters of the way, leaving a gap that gives me a sliver view of the sink *and mirror*.

I mean, we've seen all there is to see. Maybe this is normal now?

I hear the clank and thud of his shorts hitting the floor and then the metallic slide of curtain rings across the rod and back. My skin erupts in goose bumps as images of Wade, soapy and wet, bombard my brain.

"What do you think?" he calls from beneath the spray.

"I—uhh—umm—" I give up.

"Hey, Good Girl, you still out there?"

Good Girl. I'll never hear those words again without thinking of all the ways Wade and I were bad.

"Harlow?"

My head snaps up, eyes shooting to that gap from the open door and the mirror beyond. To the blue eyes watching me through the reflection.

"Fine. Yes," I answer hoarsely, no idea what I've agreed to. Not caring.

His smile spreads and then he tips his head back beneath the spray to rinse while I try to find enough air in the room to breathe.

A few minutes later, he's out of the bathroom, holding the white hotel towel at one hip while he uses another to rub his hair dry. He gives me a funny smile that's probably has something to do with me standing in exactly the same spot he left me in before he showered. "Huh."

"Huh, what?" I take two steps back. One to the side.

And realize I've moved to a spot in the room so remote and useless, it probably hasn't been occupied in all its years of existence.

"Just something Axe said." Wade's eyes flick over me, crinkling at the edges before he disappears into the front room. A minute later, I hear the pull-out groan under his weight. "Night, Good Girl. Sweet dreams."

Chapter 15

Wade

*A*ll yesterday I waited for a sign that Harlow was seeing me differently. That with time to think, she might realize she wanted more. That this thing between us was too good to cap off at one night. That a connection like ours couldn't be ignored.

Nothing.

By the end of the night, my ego was walking with a limp, complaining about the cold. My lifetime sentence to the Friend Zone about to be handed down, I was trying to be cool, because I didn't want to be the dickhead making everything weird. I didn't want to be the reason we couldn't be friends… because if that was all I could have, I'd take it.

But then we got back here.

And she got *weird*.

It was nothing I could put a finger on exactly. More like a subtle tension that hadn't been there before.

A possible weak spot to exploit.

Except I didn't want to put a move on her only to have her freak out and push me away after. I didn't want her to leave. I didn't want to lose her.

And that's when I remembered the dumbest, most asinine advice I've ever gotten.

Be the bunny.

Now it's morning and I'm in bed, thumbs grudgingly moving over my phone.

Me: Asshole.

Axe: So it worked.

I want to be mad, but damn. The look on her face last night.

Me: I thought you were fucking with me.

Axe: Yeah, I was.

I blink. Blink again. Nope, that's a twitch.

Axe: But the more I thought about it... laughing to myself for hours and hours and hours... I realized it might actually have some merit.

Me: Say goodbye to your teeth.

Axe: Nah, these chicklets are safe. You love me. And it worked.

Me: Yeah, it worked.

Axe: Not that well, if you're texting me at five in the morning. Unless her head's bobbing under the sheet. In which case, bad form, man.

Me: I'm alone. Don't be a dick.

Me: I didn't try it until late last night.

Axe: Ahh. Operator error.

I roll my eyes and send him a picture of my middle finger.

Axe: Are we done here… or were you seeking more of my wisdom?

I don't want to do it. But damn it…

Me: Have you got any bunny tips?

Axe: Hold on, let me ask Dina.

What? Two seconds later, I know.

Axe: This is D

Axe: Tp1 wrk yr mouth

Axe: lots

Axe: mve it

Axe: tuch it

Axe: bite it

Axe: open cls it evn if u dnt tlk

There's no way… except this is Axe and so yeah, it's entirely possible the person texting me is some bunny named Dina… and that until seconds ago, she was bobbing under the sheet while he texted with me.

Christ.

Axe: Tp2….

Harlow

WHAT IS WRONG WITH ME?

One night. That's all I wanted.

Some fun with a man as serious about keeping the complications out of his life as I am about keeping them out of mine.

It should have been perfect.

Six times should have been enough.

So why is it that every time I cross paths with Wade today, instead of seeing the man I respect and enjoy as much as any friend I've ever had… all I see is my own personal walking, talking Tumblr fantasy come to life?

It's not him. I mean, of course it's him. But he's not doing anything different.

He's still pulling the same boyfriend moves. Still attentive and friendly. Still making me laugh and smile.

But somehow, *everything* feels different.

From the second I peeked into the front room of the suite this morning and found him reading in bed, bare-chested, hair in such sexy disarray it was impossible to see it without imagining my fingers in it, my brain has been off.

Twitchy.

Twisting every innocent act into a moment rife with dirty potential.

It started with the bare chest and bed head, but then there was that whole business with his fork. The man was *eating*. But every time I caught a glimpse of his tongue touching the tines of his fork, dragging slow over the stainless… ugh!

His hands on the steering wheel. Yes, I know what he can do with those hands, but was the way he brushed his fingers across the leather always so pornographic?

And now, as we walk over to the pole tent set up in Janie's parents' front yard… He's held my hand a hundred times since we arrived. So why am I just now noticing that slow, circling rub he does over my knuckle?

Why, when we're surrounded by a few dozen people, am I noticing his breath against my skin when he leans in to drop a kiss at my temple? Did it always linger for that drawn-out beat? Long enough for my eyes to lift and meet his, for me to remember the rough, shuddering rush of it against my neck and ear?

And what about the heat of his body when he's behind me, hands resting over my shoulders while we chat with Janie's sister beside the pool? Did Wade standing so close always spark this low electrical charge between us, like a current that tingles and pulls and scrambles my mind so all I can think about is what it was like having him behind me Saturday night? The power of his arms holding me tight against him, the scrape of his teeth at that spot beneath where his thumb rubs small circles now... the steely thrust of his body working deep and deeper into mine until—

"*Wade.*"

The hands at my shoulders still and the conversation I wasn't following stops, confirming that sort of needy, breathless gasp wasn't isolated to my head.

"You okay, Harlow?" Wade asks, shifting me to the side so he can see my face. And yeah, that knowing smirk has flames licking up my neck and into my cheeks.

I fake-cough a couple times for my fake boyfriend and step out of his hold. "Sorry." *Cough.* "Think I need some water." *Cough, cough.* "Something in my throat."

His smirk ratchets up a notch. God, did his mouth always have that naughty slant?

I blink, shake my head, and escape to the thankfully empty kitchen for the water I don't need.

But if I thought I was getting a reprieve, I was wrong. Because sure enough, a minute later, Wade follows me in. And there's something about the way he closes the sliding glass door behind him—slowly, eyes locked with mine—that sets off another nervous flutter of wings.

He's just closing the door. Right?

And that smile. Okay, the objective part of me knows Wade's smile has been a class-five panty-melter from the start. But it didn't melt *my* panties.

Not right away.

I swallow. It does now.

Because now I know exactly what's backing it up.

"Feeling better?" he asks, strolling around the island and stopping in front of me. Too close.

Those big hands he's had all over me, *inside* me, move to my face. Rough fingers tip my head back with a touch so gentle, I have to remind myself not to lean in closer.

"You okay?"

"Y-yes. *Yes*. Needed some water. That's all."

"Sure." He's not fooled. His eyes hold with mine for another beat before he lets me go. But he doesn't move out of my space. "I'll have some too."

Reaching past me to grab his own glass, he rests a hand at my waist. His chest brushes mine, his head turning so he can drop a low, rumbly "'Scuse me" at my ear.

The air is thin, my skin hot. My voice unsteady as I ask, "What are you doing?"

Hip propped against the counter, he fills his glass from the tap.

Relaxed.

Unaffected.

"Faking it with my fake girlfriend. Same as for the last few days." That smile tips to a new degree of naughty and his voice goes conspiratorially low. "Except for those few hours when I wasn't *faking* anything at all."

Wade

I CAN'T BELIEVE I'm doing this.

But hell, if Axe is right and working my inner bunny gets Harlow thinking about my body, which leads to Harlow wanting me to get naked, and that leads to Harlow wanting me to order dinner in for a night of watching movies in my arms when we're back in Chicago, then... yeah, I'm on board.

I'll lean into the eye contact, run my hands through my hair, and find a reason to touch my bottom lip over and over—which feels fucking ridiculous, but I gotta give Dina credit, *that shit works*.

As evidenced by my mom having to say Harlow's name three times to get her attention when we first got here.

I maintain a steady flow of tips 1 through 17, mixing it up to keep things fresh. Figure out what works and what can't really be adapted for my purposes.

Tip 6. Nope.

Tip 12. *Never*.

Tip 13… Hello, little stutter Harlow just gave up followed by the breathy sound of my name. While we're *alone* in the kitchen. Yeah, this isn't for a crowd.

Riding my high of success, I pull out Dina's signature move. Tip 3.

Hooking my thumb in the pocket of my jeans, I lean back against the counter and go for it. Cocking my free arm behind my head, I stretch. Hard.

It actually feels pretty good and I'd bet I do some porn-free version of it without thinking twenty times a day. Just not while I'm subtly nudging my jeans down and arching enough to ensure I flash my happy trail when my T-shirt rides up.

Yeah, I'm that guy.

I'd be ashamed except it's hard to be humiliated when Harlow does that double take, her eyes snaring on the stretch of skin I'm "accidentally" showing off.

I've got that hard-cut vee thing going and the accompanying eight-pack because I'm fit as fuck and work my ass off for my career. But it's nice to see it paying off in other areas of my life as well.

Confident my jeans are low enough, I pull my hand from my pocket and go for the gold, adding a modified Tip 7 and doing this lazy, totally calculated back-and-forth rub across my abs. In its purest form, one would run their fingers over the swells of their tits. I've seen this one in action plenty of times and it's another move that gets results.

Jackpot!

Harlow's mouth drops open to a gratifying degree.

I give my ego a mental fist bump. We're blowing it up when I see the change.

She blinks. Lets out this delicate noise that's something between a laugh and cough. And then her eyes narrow as they coast up my chest, past the whole tight T-shirt show, to where they lock with mine.

"Wade."

Uh-Oh. That was not her nice "Wade."

My arm is down in a flash and then my arms are crossing. Shit. Is that a breeze down south?

Worried I'm not only busted, but worse, I look like some toddler with my shirt riding up my belly, I unravel my arms, smooth it down, and adjust my jeans.

"Yep?"

"Can I speak to you a moment. In private."

Considering we're standing alone in Janie's mom's kitchen, I'm assuming private means *really private*, where no one will accidentally walk in on us and hear my fake girlfriend reaming my ass out for violating the boundaries of our fake relationship.

Chapter 16

Wade

My gut feels like a bucket of pucks just landed in it as I cross to the screen door off the back of the kitchen and hold it open for Harlow.

Their backyard isn't as open as my folks'. There's a small stone terrace with a charcoal grill and a round table that seats two facing the wooded path leading down to the lake and their dock.

This has always been a happy place for me. Lots of fun memories.

Damn it, I don't want this to be where it all ends.

"Someone might come around the side," she says, and I nod, taking her hand.

"Let's walk down to the water." Only halfway there,

I change my mind, stopping at the small boathouse built off to the side of the path.

It's set into an area that's been cleared of trees and offers a rustic bench made of driftwood where we'd line up for Janie's mom to put on our sunscreen when we were kids.

As privacy goes, this is about as good as it gets. Something Harlow seems to have picked up on herself. Of course she did, because there isn't much she misses.

I'm such an ass.

I expect Harlow to sit, but instead she turns on me, eyes flashing, her finger pointed in accusation.

"What's up?" I ask, underscoring the *dumb* in dumb jock.

There's a kind of energy coming off her that has a dangerous vibe to it. Dangerous and tempting.

One shapely brow wings up. "That's how you want to play it?"

She takes a step closer, and I swear the air around her starts to pulse. I'm half expecting her hair to levitate in dark ribbons around her face.

It's *hot*.

And suddenly, I'm not worried about how pissed she is. I want it. I want her to fight. I want her to lay into me *for real*.

"What do you want me to say, Harlow? That one night was enough? It wasn't. That I've been trying to work you up? I have. That I think we're good together and this could be—"

"*No.*" She takes another step into my space, eyes searching mine. "We agreed to one night, Wade. One. I thought we were on the same page. You *said* we were on the same page."

Jesus, the way she's looking at me. Like I broke her trust.

But that's exactly what I did. "I lied. One night was never going to be enough."

She huffs, eyes turned skyward. "We've still got the better part of a week together. Don't you think it would be smarter, *safer*, not to complicate a good thing by continuing to cross the lines?"

"I think what happened between us was *fun*. I think it was hot and intense and the kind of good that casual doesn't deliver." And this time, it's me stepping into her space. "I think the second we crossed that line, *things changed*."

"They *can't* change. Even if I—" She shakes her head, hard. When her eyes come back to mine, I swear I see a flash of regret before she shuts it down. Shuts me out. "Neither one of us has room in our lives for a relationship."

It's not true. I don't have room in my life for another unwanted complication. I can't afford any more messy distractions.

But Harlow? Hell yes, I have room for her.

"Don't you remember all your rules for finding a date? There were *reasons* for them."

I stare. She has no idea.

The rules went out the window the second she said she'd come.

"I had rules too. With my own reasons for them. Wade, when I go back to work, it's not like—poof—suddenly everything's going to be different and magical, and I'm going to have room in my life for the things I didn't before. This trip is an *escape* from my reality. Temporarily. But my priorities haven't changed."

Jesus. How did I not see this?

I may have broken mine, but Harlow has stuck to her rules from the start.

What happened between us was her taking a break from her life, giving in to some fun. The kind she never lets herself have because it doesn't align with her goals. She's a dedicated workaholic and she likes it that way.

Except that she *doesn't*.

Not really.

What did she say to me? That being herself was exhausting.

I've never once heard her say how much she loves her job. How satisfying it is to work fifteen-hour days seven days a week. How graduating high school two years early and finishing college in three gave her a sense of fulfillment like she'd never known. How the trade-off of everything she's sacrificed in her life is so totally worth it.

And whatever it is that happened back at the bank the day we met at the club—she'd been devastated by it. But that's what she's telling me she wants to go back to.

A life where she never says yes. Where she doesn't smile or laugh. Where the guys she dates care more about her old man than they do her.

That's—that's a fucking travesty.

It's not my place to tell her how to run her life or what her priorities are. Who the fuck am I to tell her anything? No.

But maybe… it doesn't have to be over just yet.

Maybe we can have this week. Maybe if I back off some, ask for less, she'll keep letting me be the fun she so desperately needs for a few more days.

And maybe it will be enough for Harlow to see that, even if she doesn't want me, she wants more from her life than she's been letting herself have.

"Fine, your priorities haven't changed. But your escape isn't over. We've got the rest of the week. Why start saying 'no' to the good times we could have when there's still time to say 'yes'?"

Her shoulders fall. "Because it can't last."

It could. If she'd let it.

"So what if it doesn't?" I shrug like it's no big deal, like there's nothing to lose. I'm a damn liar. "We'll have this week."

I take a step closer, let my eyes rake over her body. "I'll have more of how wet you get for me, how hard you come, and the way you look at me when I'm buried deep and hard inside you. You'll have more of what none of those fucking *suits* could give you."

Her eyes are wide, her breath pulling in slowly.

"You know what I keep thinking about?" I should stop. Shut the hell up. But instead, I take another step into that charged space between us, leaving barely an inch for the air to crackle. "What you'll taste like if we have another chance. Your fingers in my hair as I give you my mouth. Your knees shaking at my shoulders as you come on my tongue."

I can't stop thinking about how limp she goes after I make her scream and how good it feels when I pull her over me and our hearts slow together. That minute when it feels like she's mine. "You know it's good."

Her teeth catch the full swell of her bottom lip, and she peers up at me through the thick fringe of lashes.

I wait for the words I don't want to hear. That I need to get over myself and there won't be any repeats of Saturday.

Her hands come up, and I brace for a shove back into my own space if I'm lucky, a slap for running my mouth if I'm not. She makes a fist… and a hot second later my brain registers that it's in my shirt, *and she's not pushing me away*.

Harlow

I'M CRAZY. That's the only explanation for why I've got my hands in Wade's shirt and my body pressed against his as I open beneath the crush of his kiss. Why I'm moaning around the possessive thrust of his tongue and melting into the strength of his hold.

I should be telling him that what happened between us was a mistake. That it can't happen again. But the only words finding their way from my lips to his are fractured pleas, increasing in desperation with every heated second that passes.

The arms around me wrap impossibly tighter and my feet leave the ground. The world spins, and then my back meets the worn wood siding of the boathouse protecting us from prying eyes. My legs lock around his hips as Wade rocks into me, hitting the achy spot that has my belly twisting in on itself, hard.

Breathless, I pull back to meet his eyes. "Wade, this can't be the start of something."

He stares at me for a beat, the shadows in the fading

light making it impossible to read his eyes. But then his head jerks in a short nod, and he's got the door open beside us.

Our mouths fuse in another hungry kiss, and holding me like I weigh nothing, Wade carries me into the relative darkness of the small building. The door latches and we're all over each other. Frantic. Hands everywhere, breaths coming sharp and hard.

He's got both hands on my ass, gripping me with a sexy, possessive hold that has me moaning into his mouth. I've never kissed with such raw and unscripted desire. There's nothing careful or deliberate about what's happening here, and it's incredible.

Lowering me to stand, he guides me to the wall.

"Lean back. Yeah, like this." Then, eyes locked with mine, he goes to his knees.

Big hands smooth over my calves and then higher up the backs of my thighs. "Lift your dress for me, Good Girl."

Achy need grips my center and, hands shaking, I do as he asks and lift it. God, there's nothing good about what I'm doing here... except how it feels.

His touch gentles as he helps me with my panties, pocketing them once they're free.

"Give me your leg," he says, drawing it forward and draping it over his shoulder. He groans, licking his lips.

And just when the heat from his eyes feels like it's

going to burn right through me, he leans in and kisses me.

The first soft touch pulls a shocked breath from me, and my hands fly to his head, holding him back.

What am I doing?

Blue eyes meet mine. "No?"

Heat blazes through me in a mix of embarrassment and desire. "We shouldn't do this. What if—?"

"What if I spoil you so good you never get off without thinking about my mouth again?" He drags his bottom lip through his teeth. "It's inevitable. Go with it."

This man. "What if someone hears us?"

"I'll be quiet." He winks. "Promise."

A huff of laughter escapes. *"I'll bet."*

But he's done waiting. "You're gonna want to hold on for this."

And then he gives me the slowest, longest, most incredibly thorough kiss of my life.

Licking his lips, he looks up at me with hooded eyes. "So fucking sweet."

I'm not breathing.

He nuzzles into the slickness between my legs, kissing me again and again. Teasing me with his lips, his tongue. Soft and then firm and then, God, I don't even know what he's doing, but it's—

I gasp, my fingers closing in his hair.

"You like that, Good Girl?" he growls against me. "You like my mouth on your sweet pussy?"

I don't know if I actually answer with words, but his rough chuckle tells me he understands all the same.

His right arm loops beneath my thigh, his hand closing over my hip to pull me closer, open me more.

My head rocks back against the wall, my eyes squinting closed as he works me with dirty praise and promises.

"So wet for me... So hot."

Teases me with his lips, his teeth.

"Could eat you for days... That's it, Good Girl..."

With deep, penetrating thrusts of his tongue and slow, swirling licks that have need spearing through me, sharp and sweet.

This is amazing. So good.

Drugging and addictive.

I'm almost there. That needy coil so tight within me I'm mindless.

So close.

And then he's circling my opening with the blunt end of his finger.

"Please," I gasp, rocking into the touch.

He sinks deep and I stop breathing.

"Feel so good, Harlow. So slick and soft."

Flicking his tongue against me, he pumps his fingers in time. "So tight."

"Don't stop."

"Never gonna stop." He gives me another finger, stretching me so I clench and spasm around him. "Never gonna get enough of your sweetness."

"More," I beg, my body so far gone there's nothing but Wade and his mouth and this storm within me that's about to break.

"Want to give you more." His fingers meet that spot deep inside with a soft caress as he brushes his lips against my clit. "Want to give you everything."

I'm nodding, desperate.

"One more night won't be enough for all the fun we could have—"

He vees his fingers and twists.

"Let me make it good—" Another circling stroke of his tongue takes me to the edge and then stops short. Has me clutching at his hair, pushing my hips into the contact I can't get enough of.

I'm shaking, burning up. My body in a rebellion like I've never known.

Wade pulls back, his mouth hovering a breath away from relief. "Give me the week, Good Girl."

"Anything." Anything he wants.

His fingers crook, finding that spot again and pressing. "Say it, Harlow. A week. *Give it to me.*"

"Yes—Wade—please—*a week!*"

I catch the flash of his cocky smirk before his lips close around my clit and *he sucks*.

Every part of my being pulls in, concentrating and coalescing for a weighted beat before I come apart with a blistering intensity that goes on and on and on. He holds me tight, keeping me from collapsing as wave after wave of cresting pleasure rips through me. Until the world around me hazes out and there's nothing but Wade's deep voice rumbling against me.

"Mine. One week, Harlow."

Chapter 17

Harlow

"It does too count," Wade growls against my neck as we're standing in the back of the living room watching Janie opening wedding gifts.

His arms are snug around my waist, holding me so my back is tight to his front.

"I was under duress."

The light scrape of his stubble tickles my neck, making me wonder what it's done to my skin in other places. My legs press together and I have to bite my lip from how sensitive I am.

How much I want him again.

All of him.

Wade stills behind me, his breath coming in a warm

rush. I can feel the smile on his lips. "Time to go, Good Girl."

Silently, I nod.

This is madness.

Wade edges past me and cuts over to where his mom is standing. A few quick words, then he's tugging me outside, and we're running for the truck. He throws the door open and before I can blink, he's got me by the waist, lifting me into the passenger seat.

Laughing, I push at my dress to keep it from riding up. But Wade has other ideas.

He bites his bottom lip and pulls it through the sexy clasp of his teeth. "One look."

"Not on your life!"

Only he's nodding, that gleam in his eyes as naughty as I've ever seen. "They're all *ooh*ing and *ahh*ing over Janie's new Instant Pot, but even if they checked outside, all they'll see is the open door and my back. Come on. One peek."

My eyes flare wide and, laughing, I check over his shoulder to the house filled with family and friends. "Absolutely not."

His hands creep higher and beneath the dome light, I can see the hint of his tongue against the spot he just bit.

He is so… crazy… hot. My legs widen.

Satisfaction lights his eyes as his thumbs skate over the still bare, sensitive skin of my sex.

Someone wouldn't give me my panties back after the boathouse.

"One more taste, Harlow." He leans in, urging my knees apart with those big hands to make room for his even bigger body. "I'm *starving*."

I'm shaking my head the entire time, and I'm pretty sure somewhere deep inside there's a part of me that really wants him to stop. But she's not the one breathless and leaning back over the center console, sliding one knee fractionally higher. She's not the one watching as he pushes my dress aside so I'm open and exposed to him again. So that we can both see when he drags his thumb through my slickness in one stroke… and then, eyes blazing, brings it to his mouth.

"Wade," I manage on a broken breath.

"Yeah, Good Girl?"

"What do we have on the calendar for tomorrow?"

His brow arches, the corner of his mouth kicking up with it. "Errand in the city, but pretty easy day."

"Good." Hooking my fingers in his jeans pocket, I tug him closer. "Because you're not getting any sleep tonight. Now get in the truck."

Wade

A BOSSY HARLOW is a sexy Harlow.

Almost as sexy as playful, teasing Harlow.

But nothing compares to *daring* Harlow.

When she opens her legs for me while I'm driving down that dark, deserted backroad outside of town and lets me slide my finger deep, in and out, until she comes apart all over my hand… Jesus.

I almost lose it right there.

But even going thirteen miles an hour for half the ride, we eventually make it back. And then up to our room, where I have Harlow against the door—*inside* our room, but barely—on the desk, the bed—not the pull-out—beneath the shower and, for a while, on the floor with my back against the inside of the closet.

I get my mouth on her again, and with the number of times I make her moan, my ego should be wearing a super-suit and flexing in front of a mirror. Instead, he's flipping a puck on his stick, staring at me expectantly.

What are you going to do, Wade?

Yeah, I got Harlow to agree to the full week. But even if she actually gives it to me—and that's a pretty big *if*, considering she sort of *was* under duress—she's going to be worried about after.

Which is why, after giving my body a workout more

intense than any game I've played in pro hockey, instead of sleeping, I'm awake, running my fingers through the dark silk of her hair as she sleeps against my chest.

I must finally drift off, because the next time I open my eyes, it's to a room bright with sunshine streaming in around the drapes and Harlow watching me with sleepy eyes from my chest.

My heart does something I haven't ever felt before. It's so good, so full it almost hurts.

"Okay. One week," she says softly.

Taking her arms, I haul her up my chest.

We'll start with one. But I'm going to make it so good, no fucking way will she want it to end.

Harlow

FOR ALL MY RESISTANCE, I'm already seeing the benefits of being Wade Grady's temporarily real, fake girlfriend. The man has been holding back in no small way. But now that he's not skating the line between real and fake, it's like some restrictor has come off. And this Wade is *undiluted*, pure dirty-talking charm and charisma.

This Wade doesn't keep his hands above my waist or limit our contact.

This Wade doesn't just wrap his arms around me from behind... he buries his face in that spot between my shoulder and neck and does this low growl thing that has me squirming in his arms and the poor couple in the elevator with us laughing into their hands.

This Wade throws me over his shoulder and carts me, wriggling and squealing, across the hotel lot to the grassy strip where we stretch before our run.

This Wade watches me with the kind of heat and intensity that leaves me a little breathless and a lot hot... and wondering what kind of defense I would have had if he'd shown me this true side of him from the start. *Not enough.*

"Keep looking at me like that, Good Girl, and you can forget running out to the orchard. The only workout you're getting today is back in that bed." He does that lip-biting thing again, but this time there's nothing scripted about it. It's *authentic* as his eyes rake shamelessly over the length of my legs, fixing on my running shorts-covered ass.

I shiver, averting my eyes and grinning down at my shoes.

It isn't until we start our run that things fall back into place. But now that they have, I'm more focused on what Wade is sharing about his career than I am on the way the boulder-like muscles of his thighs shift and flex with every step he takes.

"I guess I assumed it was a pretty straightforward ascent once you made the move from football to hockey."

Wade lets out a laugh, keeping pace beside me, his breath even and strong. "Not me. Lots of guys get picked up right out of high school. You know Greg Baxter?"

I read a bit about him while researching the team. "He was your captain but retired because of a concussion, right?"

"Yeah, well, that guy's career trajectory was like a rocket. Mine was more like those terraced rice fields cut into the mountains in Japan. From a natural talent standpoint, guys like Baxter have me beat hands down."

I slant him a look, doubtful. "But here you are. Playing at the same level."

Another laugh. "Because I never fucking quit. Yeah, I got here. But if I'd let up for even a minute, I wouldn't have." We round a bend in the gravel road and the big painted sign for the orchard comes into view. "I played in college, but not on a free ride. Coach told me once he'd never expected me to advance past that level."

"What?"

"Yeah, but I busted my ass, studied every tape, talked my way into more practice, more ice time, more one-on-one. And I made sure that every game I played reminded the decision-makers that they wanted me to play more in the next. I'm not a finesse guy, but I get it done. And that's how I got myself into the AHL, how I earned the game time there, the chance for Taxi Squad. More time playing up than down." He shakes his head. "But this was the first full season I've played with the Slayers."

And from the articles, it sounds like he's impressed everyone. "I read that your contract is up for renewal."

"They're hammering it out now. It'll be finalized in the next couple weeks. Deadline's at the end of the month." Wade slows to a walk. Stops and turns to me. "Signing my first endorsement helps too. Good press. Good season for me even if it wasn't great for the team. The stuff happening now—it's a big deal for me. No matter how hard I worked, I knew the odds were against me getting here."

I nod, my throat inexplicably tight. This man is nothing like I'd assumed that first night in the club. He's driven, intelligent, kind and humble in the most unexpected ways. He knows what it means to work for something you may not get and to keep going anyway.

"But now you have. It must feel amazing."

He lets out a laugh, kicking at the dirt. "It feels

fucking fragile. Like finally, I ought to be able to take a breath, but I can't. Not if I want to hold on to what I've been killing myself to get."

"Wade." I want to step into his body, take his face in my hands, and—I don't even understand what I'm feeling except that it's a pull I can't give in to.

"Don't give me that gentle voice, like you're sorry for me, Good Girl." He offers a lopsided smile so different from his sexy smirk, something melts inside me. "I'm exactly where I want to be. This is what I signed up for. And no matter who you are or how you got there, if you're in the NHL, your clock is ticking. You're always fighting to keep your spot."

"Well, I hope you get to keep it for a long time."

"So," he drawls, stepping in closer. "You know about my contract. Been studying up on my sport pretty hard?" He picks up a bit of my hair and starts playing with it. The touch is so teasing and light, goose bumps break out across my skin. "Think you'd be interested in seeing a game?"

In this moment, it's like there's nothing fake between us. Never has been. It tightens my chest in a way that has nothing to do with the miles we've run.

"You could sit in my seats," he says, voice low and rough.

I swallow. Feel my heart turn over in my chest. I can't go to his game. We won't be together.

"Wear my number."

But even knowing it won't happen, I can almost see it.

"I'll knock the glass when I skate by, warming up."

How did we get this close?

I'd swear he didn't move, but my head is tipped back and he's staring down at me.

"I'll show off for you. Score for you. Take you out after to meet the team."

But if he wasn't the one to breach my space then I must have—

His mouth closes over mine, slow and sweet.

When he pulls back, it's with a smile that makes me ache.

"You're thinking too hard. It's just a game, Harlow." He gives that bit of hair a gentle tug and lets it unravel from his finger.

"I know, but when this week is over—"

"We can't even be friends?" He asks it so casually, but there's something in the way he's watching me that says he's not so casual at all.

I could say yes. Tell him what he wants to hear. But I know what it feels like to be strung along, and it stinks.

I could tell him no. Leave no room for misunderstanding. But even though there's no romantic future for us, the idea of not having this man's friendship feels bad in a way that steals my breath.

Moving off the road, I sit on the soft grass beside the fence. I stretch my legs out in front of me while Wade sits beside me and hangs his arms over his spread knees.

"Come on, Good Girl. Lay it on me."

Chapter 18

Harlow

"I'd like to be friends with you." I'd like to be able to see his smile and hear that gruff laugh. "But it can't be friends like we're friends now." He can't play with my hair or make me feel like I'm the only thing he sees. "What we're doing this week… it has to end here."

He looks past me into the morning sun.

"Why?" And then before I can answer he adds, "I'm not arguing with you. I'm asking, because I don't get it."

That's the thing. I don't think most people would. No matter how I tried to explain. But Wade? I think he might.

"You know how you were with hockey, where you

wanted it even though your coaches maybe didn't see your potential until you proved it?"

Some of the light leaves his eyes. "Yeah."

"My career goals come with their own set of obstacles. Not everyone sees my potential. I'm young—"

"You're smart as hell with a handful of degrees to back it up."

"Thank you. But I've already been boxed out of the job I've invested a lot of time and energy in." Years of experience, trainings, and certifications at every turn.

"What happened?"

"I'd been offered a promotion to head up the division. But at the last minute, they did some restructuring and brought someone else in."

He coughs, eyes narrowing. "Someone with more experience?"

If only. Someone with more *entitlement*.

"Someone with a better relationship with the person making the decisions."

"So now you work for this… *guy*?"

He thinks it's about me being a woman. That there's a boys' club behind my problems. Who knows, maybe that's part of it. But not all. Not even most.

"No. I don't work for him. We'd already backfilled my position with someone who moved from out of state. I became a redundancy."

"The fuck, Harlow?" he demands, outraged on my behalf. "They can't do that, can they? Does HR know?"

It feels like everyone knows.

"There are a number of issues complicating the situation. But no. This avenue of advancement isn't an option anymore. Which means what I do now matters. I can't afford to drop the ball. So no distractions. No conflicts. No mistakes."

"This guy in charge. He still going to have a say in your advancement?"

"Yes." And that's the point. "He's at the top of the food chain."

"You should definitely take my seats. Invite him to a game."

I lean a shoulder into Wade. He's strong and solid and warm. "If only it were that simple."

"Don't tell me he doesn't like hockey."

Shaking my head, I take a deep breath. Dig deep to keep my voice level. "He doesn't like *me*."

He's quiet beside me. Then, "Why the hell not?"

And the way he says it, like it's not possible, like it's so far outside the realm of possibility that someone wouldn't like me… It's really nice.

"No idea." That's the truth. Part of it anyway. "It's been like that from the start. Something about me rubs him the wrong way, I guess."

"Why would you want to work for a guy like that?

You could change banks. They have compliance departments everywhere, don't they?"

I meet his eyes. "But *this* is the bank I care about."

"So what you're saying is you really, *really* needed this vacation."

I laugh, and it feels good after a conversation it hurts to have.

"Seriously, let me know if you want seats."

He lays another quick, hard kiss on me, then pulls me up and challenges me to a race back.

Wade

I'D LIKE to say I let her win, but Harlow guts it out fair and square, making it back to the hotel besting me by less than a two-foot lead.

Damn, she's intense.

I reward her with the first turn under the shower spray and a full body wash so thorough and complete, *I'm* rewarded with my name echoing off the walls as I get her dirty all over again.

We have breakfast at the bakery in town. Harlow wants to hear more about the team, and I tell her about the guys I play with. I give up the stories I know will make her laugh, even the ones that make me look like a tool. But I can't stop thinking about her job. I hate the idea of her getting screwed over like that. And more, I hate the idea of what she'll be going back to when this trip is over.

I can relate to going after something not everyone believes is within my reach. But at least when I prove I can deliver, *I get to keep the job*.

After breakfast, we drive out to the city to pick up the place cards from one of Janie's aunts. My mom tried to talk me into leaving Harlow behind to hang out with her—and I get it, we all want more of her—but she's mine, and I'm not giving up a minute I don't have to.

We hold hands in the truck.

I make her laugh and make her blush and ask her a million questions.

On the way back, we ride long stretches with a kind of comfortable silence between us I'm not used to. It's nice. It makes me want to take her to the hotel and pull her into my arms for more.

But my mom is waiting, so we head to my parents' place instead.

"These turned out so pretty," my mom coos, checking over the hand-done calligraphy with Harlow at what used to be our dining room table. Currently, it's covered with every kind of crafting DIY supply you can imagine.

"What's with the hot glue gun?"

She rolls her eyes and laughs like I'm pulling her leg.

Harlow gives up one of those soft smiles that's somehow twice as potent as its full-bodied counterpart.

Then she's offering to help with the "embellishments," and even though I don't know what the hell that means, I'm assuming it's this arts-and-crafts stuff. "Yeah, I'll help too."

Both women turn to me with raised brows.

Okay, so my hands are twice as big as theirs, but I think I can handle some glitter and sticking a few of those beady things to a card.

"Wade, honey, you don't have to help. Why don't you call your brother or Tommy? Relax a while."

Harlow bites her lip against a smile. So cute.

"Nah, I'll help."

She peers up at me. "When was the last time you did anything crafty?"

"Art class in high school."

My mother's hand moves to her hip, her eyes going narrow. "You got a C."

Harlow coughs, her eyes going wide like she's just uncovered my greatest shame and doesn't quite know how to face me.

Jesus.

"C-plus."

"Only because Sandy White did half your projects."

How the hell does Mom know that?

I straighten, digging in because I can't fucking help it. "The bad half."

And then I'm pulling out my chair and sitting down. End of discussion.

Two hours later, I'm going blind beneath the glare of my mother's makeup mirror, my two favorite women in my face, both fussing at once.

"I told you not to touch your eyes."

"Jesus, it's in his ear."

"Have you seen *his hair*?"

"We may have to cut that out."

I try to push them away—gently—but my mother says my name in that way that has me slumping back.

"It was an *accident*," I groan.

"We have more glue, honey."

"I can drive back out for more of those card things."

Harlow pauses from working the coconut oil into my face. "This one's like a glittery beauty mark. I kind of want to leave it."

They both fall into another bout of teary-eyed laughter, and suddenly, I don't really mind at all.

When they can breathe again, my mom pats my chest and then sighs at the fresh coating of glitter on her hand. "Honey, don't worry about the place cards. I only gave you the ones for the guests that canceled after we placed the order."

"*What?*"

My mom points at my left eye. "Get his lashes."

I'm sentenced to a shower, but first I'm forced to endure the indignity of standing in the backyard while my mom empties a can of Aqua Net, spraying down my clothes. I don't even get to use my own shower, instead being banished to the first-floor shoebox off the utility room where I strip and hand my glitter-coated, hairspray-soaked clothing to Harlow through the door.

After washing my hair with olive oil and then a crusty bottle of baby shampoo I suspect has been squatting under our sink for the last twenty-five years, I dry off with a torn towel from the rag pile. When I'm done, there's a neat stack of folded clothes waiting outside the door, probably left behind from my college days.

I pull them on and mutter a curse.

Mom and Harlow are in the dining room, their backs to me, the glitter miraculously contained to the tiny bowls of its origin.

Standing in the doorway, I wait for them to notice me. And when they do, it's everything I'd hoped for.

Harlow catches me in the corner of her eye and turns with a smile that goes slack as her eyes drop south to the sweatpants so snug they've got to be two sizes too small and… make everything under them look two sizes too big.

"Umm, Wade…"

"Yeah, babe?"

My mom turns. Her eyes bug and then squint shut as she throws her hand out to block her view. "Jesus, *Wade*!"

Uh-huh. "I'm going back to the hotel to grab some clothes."

Hand still blocking her view, my mom fumbles out of her seat. "You aren't leaving this house, mister. If Kelsey comes home from the courthouse early, lock yourself in your room." Then to Harlow, "Grab his keys, we'll get his clothes."

Harlow

I MAKE it all the way to the truck before I crack. Grace slides into the passenger seat beside me, the horror still lingering in her eyes. She takes my hand in hers and we both fold forward, laughing so hard I'm not sure it will ever stop.

"I've never seen anything so—"

"He should have warned us—"

"Were those even his?"

Grace wipes her eyes and sits back. "I thought so, but maybe they were Walt's?"

I shake my head. "From middle school?"

She scrunches her face in thought. "I don't *think* so?"

And I die laughing some more.

I get a text from Wade telling me the circulation is being cut off to my favorite "fun park" and to put the truck in gear and go. After adjusting every setting six hundred times, it's about as good as it's going to get.

"I don't normally drive Wade's truck. Are you sure you want to come along?"

Grace buckles up. "Absolutely. You see what I have to deal with raising these boys? I'll take every minute with their girls I can get."

I don't wreck the truck and Grace waits in the lot while I grab the clothes. Grace peppers me with stories about Wade as a boy, and I'm grinning so hard I'm pretty sure I'm going to have to ice my cheeks from the workout they're getting.

When we get back, Walt's car is in the drive and I can only imagine his reaction to his brother's nothing-left-to-the-imagination ensemble.

But when we walk in, it's not Walt I see.

"*David?*" I choke out.

Chapter 19

Harlow

"Harlow Richards, what the heck?" David chuckles, rushing over to shake my hand with both of his. "This is unexpected. How do you know Walt?"

I blink, holding my smile in place as my worlds collide.

A warm hand smooths over my back, circling around to my hip in a possessive hold. And my breath stalls in my lungs, any hope—irrational as it might have been—of keeping David Carlson from human resources at PHR from finding out who I'm here with goes out the window.

His brows bump to his hairline. "You're Wade's—" He turns to Wade, who's still wearing the obscene sweats, not that anyone's paying attention now. "Wow, man. I had no idea. When did this happen?"

My heart starts to pound and my mind spins.

When *did* this start? What did we agree to say? Are we both about to be caught?

"It's pretty new," Wade offers casually, rubbing his hand over my side. "We've been trying to keep it quiet, off social, you know."

"Right, that makes sense." He leans in and gives me a conspiratorial wink that has Wade's hand stilling where it is. "Harlow, I assure you, no one's going to hear it from me. Just gotta make sure we don't end up in any of the same pictures. Plausible deniability, right?"

Wade frowns.

But then Grace is edging past me. "Davey, come here."

His face splits into a wide grin as he steps into her hug.

Everyone starts talking at once, about the drive down, wedding prep, Wade's sweatpants, and the "trouser snake" Walt can't unsee.

Grace shoos her oldest off to change and ushers everyone into the kitchen, where she pulls a pitcher of tea from the fridge. I get the glasses down and hand them out as she pours.

When Wade reemerges, he's wearing the cargo

shorts and T-shirt I picked for him. I hand him a glass and tuck myself into his side. The smile he gives me as he pulls me closer isn't that far off from the ones he's given me while we were deep in the *fake*, but somehow it feels completely different.

All grins, Grace pats the counter. "So talk about a small world. How do you two know each other now?"

This is not a big deal. "David and I both work at PHR."

David's head bobs. "I'm in HR, so we don't work together. But of course"—he shoots me a smile—"I know *her*."

Walt raises a brow, the corner of his mouth twitching as he exchanges a look with his brother. I want to tell Wade it's not what he's thinking—that there's nothing between us. Because the possessive way his arm circles around me says he's thinking there is.

Grace's lips purse. "Harlow, honey, I know you said banking. But what do you do there?"

My belly drops. David knows. I can't just brush over it. If I say I'm still working in compliance, it will seem like I'm embarrassed and lying. There's no other choice. "I'm sort of between positions right now."

And those muttered apologies make it even worse. "No, it's not—"

David shakes his head with a laugh. "Grace, she's

fine. 'Between positions' isn't the same when your dad owns the bank."

Wade chokes into his tea and David's eyes bug, all the color leaving his face. "Dude, you didn't know her dad owns the bank?"

My boyfriend should totally know.

Real or fake. I should have mentioned it earlier, and now—

"*What?* No, man, of course I knew." Wade chuckles from behind me, easy as can be. "New to the whole swallowing thing."

Walt snorts and Grace rolls her eyes, knowing exactly what her youngest is thinking. Wade steps away from me, wiping his chin with the back of his arm. He's only setting his glass in the sink. That's all. It's reasonable. Normal.

Except Wade is so good at weaving fiction into the fabric of what's real. What if he's not just putting his glass away? What if he's upset because I didn't trust him with the truth?

A cold sort of dread snakes through my belly, different than the one that lives there most of the time. This one feels… worse.

I watch the muscles of his back as he washes his hands. He turns around, drying his hands. "It's no big deal about the bank. But not what we lead with, you know."

David gulps air, looking more relieved than I feel. Grace waves her hand in the air, moving on.

It's very polite, and I'm trying to be polite too. Trying not to give in to this almost soul-deep pull to go to Wade. To make sure we're okay. Which is ridiculous because this thing between us is only a week. It's not real in a way that should matter.

But it does.

It matters. And when he crosses back to me, brushing a light kiss at the corner of my mouth, my breath rushes out in relief. And then he's holding me close again, and I'm turning, wrapping my arms around his middle to hold him tighter still.

It's only a week. But I don't want to give up a second of it.

Wade

WE HANG out at the house for a while. Catch up with Dave, share my snafu with the place cards, and hear about Janie's cousin who eloped this past weekend. Harlow stays close to my side, but it's not enough. I want to be alone with her. After what I'm calling a reasonable amount of time passes, I pull her to her feet and tuck her into my side.

"Guys, we'll see you later. I've got a call with my agent in not too long, so we're going to cut out." It's true-ish. The call isn't actually for another couple hours.

Mom nods, grabbing a baby carrot from the dip plate she set out. "Don't forget your clothes from the dryer."

Right. We grab my stuff and head out, but don't even make it to the walk before Dave's behind us.

"Harlow, you have a second?" he asks, following us down the front step.

I don't like the way her body gets tense every time this guy opens his mouth.

"Of course. What's on your mind?"

She sounds crisp, professional. I've heard it before, but I haven't seen this side of Harlow since we arrived in town. And it's a little weird, but not nearly so much as seeing that polite professionalism from the kid who stuffed French fries up his nose when he was ten.

"I've been meaning to tell you how sorry I am about the way things shook out with your brother. Everyone knows that job should have been yours."

Her *brother* is the guy who got her job.

And her dad owns the bank.

I don't want to believe it. I don't want Harlow's father to be the man she doesn't think likes her. It's possible it's an uncle, another relation. But my gut doesn't think so.

Beside me, Harlow smiles a workplace smile. But it's not *real*.

"Thank you for saying so, but I'm certain Junior will do a terrific job. We're happy to have him back on board."

Damn.

Once I've got her in the truck with my parents' place in the rearview, I ask, *"Junior?"*

She laughs softly, shaking her head. "I thought when he started working he'd go by Philip—but no. He's a Junior, through and through."

"Sounds like an asshole."

"I mean, he kind of is." She takes a breath, lets it out. "He's self-centered, entitled, elitist. But he's not a terrible person. He's just kind of… careless. And because of who he is, he gets away with it."

We come up to the intersection and instead of turning left, I go right, taking us away from town.

I expect Harlow to ask about it. No way she didn't notice, but she's quiet, holding my hand as we drive a few miles into the country. I pull down the dusty gravel road, wondering if the kids still come out here.

We pass a small, dark house with a broken window, an overgrown yard, and a handful of dilapidated outbuildings before I pull to a stop in front of the old sway-back barn.

"What's this?" Harlow asks as I help her out of the truck and pull a Slayers blanket from the back.

"Another quiet spot."

"Good for thinking?" she asks, holding my hand as I lead her around the side.

"Good for *talking*." And because I can feel her on the brink of asking, I tell her. "I might have brought a girl or two out here… back in the day."

She laughs, and the sound of it warms me from the inside.

When we get to the clearing past the building, she stops, her breath catching in a pretty way.

"I was hoping they still did this." The back side of the barn is the only part of the property that's seen a fresh coat of paint in probably twenty years. Maybe more. "Every year, the seniors paint the back with something significant to their class—the science lab with the empty desk is about Mrs. Green retiring—and those squares along the bottom are individual student quotes or tags."

"They did this when you were in high school?"

"Yep." I find a spot beneath an old oak, kicking a bit through the field grass to check for broken glass or anything I wouldn't want Harlow sitting on, but the kids must have maintained the tradition of cleaning up whatever mess they bring in as well.

She helps me spread the blanket and we stretch out.

"Bet you can't guess what they painted my year."

"Hockey stick? You scoring with your parents weeping in the stands?"

"You'd think, right?" My girl is catering to my ego. Will wonders never cease? "Actually, it was a football jersey with Jordan Jamison's name and number. He took us to State."

She pulls a pout. "Enderson sure loves their football."

"Got that right."

I fold one arm behind my head and draw Harlow in with the other so she's tucked into my side, her hand flat over my heart.

It feels good.

"How about you? What did you put in your square?"

"'If you want something, work for it. If you don't get it, work harder.' One of those unknown-origin quotes off the internet, but I had it taped into my locker for about six years."

She peers at me, the softest smile on her lips. "That's so you. I love it."

I hold her tighter.

After another minute, she takes a deep breath. Bracing. And I know she's ready to talk.

"I wasn't trying to hide who I was from you. It's just… I didn't think it would come up. Most people don't know his name. And I guess I didn't want to have to answer all the usual questions. I didn't want to tell you what it's like working for him or whether he's proud to have me following in his footsteps."

That quiet admission kills me. Makes me struggle to keep my hold loose and my breath even. She doesn't need to be trying to calm my ass down.

"Your dad's the one you… don't have a good relationship with? The one you want to prove yourself to."

"It wasn't easy telling you that stuff." She buries her face in my side and gives another small laugh, this one missing any trace of humor at all. "But it was way easier without you knowing who he was to me."

"Hey, come on, Harlow," I urge gently. "Don't hide."

"It's so embarrassing. Wade, everyone knows what happened. I've been working at corporate in one capacity or another since I was sixteen, and I've never let on about the issues with my father. Until this, no one knew. And now… everyone does."

There's nothing I can say to ease that sting. Dave's show of support this afternoon probably only served to underscore that greater hurt. The one that's less about the job and more about her colleagues witnessing the lack of respect her own father showed her. There's nothing to make it better. But I tell her anyway. "I'm so sorry. I wish you didn't have to go through that." Then, "Did something happen between you and your dad?"

Chapter 20

Wade

"It's going to sound so melodramatic, but so far as I can tell, my first affront was being born."

"What?"

"He only married my mother because he had to. He didn't know much about her, from what I understand, and they didn't spend much time together before she was killed. And after, he—" She sits up and shrugs. "He traveled, and with the hours he worked, he mostly stayed in the city, so I didn't see a lot of him."

I'm afraid to ask. "Who took care of you?"

"Nannies, mostly. But later"—she smiles, meeting my eyes—"teachers."

The kind of people who dedicate their careers to

providing approval for a job well done. I've got a new understanding of why Harlow is so driven to excel. And it breaks my damn heart.

"How did you end up working at the bank?" Maybe her father saw it as a way to relate to her, at least initially.

"Ignorance?" She bites her lip. "Defiance? I'd been waiting to turn sixteen, thinking once I was old enough to work, I'd be able to get a job there. The bank was so important to him, you know? It was everything. So I asked him about it, and he told me there wasn't a position."

Fucking *bastard*.

"*Our* bank. One of the largest in the United States. But nothing available. I was at the top of my class. You'd think I'd have understood. He didn't want me. But then, I had sixteen years of practice ignoring the obvious."

I think about the way Harlow smiles when my mom pulls her in for a hug or how hard she laughed when my dad tried to show her how to throw a football, and it kills me to think that she never had that. That she was following after this man, practically pleading for his affection. And from the looks of it, she's never gotten it.

But I want to know the rest. I want to understand her. "So how'd you end up working there?"

Wrapping her arms around her legs, she rests her

cheek on her knees to look at me. "I figured if there wasn't anything available, I'd make sure my name was on the list. I went to my father's building and gave my name at the front desk, asking if there was anyone in HR I could speak to about filling out an application."

"They recognized your name."

A nod. "Next thing I knew, one of David's predecessors was skittering out of the elevator to escort me upstairs so I could fill out an application. They probably thought it was adorable. I'm sure they had no idea that finding me that first position might have put their own jobs at risk."

All she needed was a way in. So smart and driven. There would have been no stopping her. "How'd he take it when you told him the good news?"

"He just stared at me for a minute. Annoyed. But then he said, 'Fine. Don't expect any special treatment. You won't get it.'"

"Nice guy." I shake my head. "Is he like that with your brother?"

"Oh, no way. Junior's the family he always wanted. He loves him. Loved Sandy—that's Junior's mother." Then raising a brow at me, I see a glint of humor in her eyes. "She *left* him."

Serves the guy right. "Yeah?"

"For *Gordon LeMere*."

I choke, eyes bugging wide. "The *hockey player*?" The

guy was at the peak of his career in the early nineties, but he retired before I laced up my first pair of skates.

And then it clicks.

"Holy shit, Good Girl. You were really, *really* pissed when he gave that job to your brother."

This time the laugh she gives up is pure Harlow. I reach for her and, pulling her into my lap, kiss the shriek off her lips. "So you've been using me this whole time, huh? Revenge is best served on a hockey stick?"

And now I get why she'd been so sure her father wouldn't like me. Why seats to my game weren't going to get her anywhere.

"I wasn't planning to serve it at all. Knowing how much he'd hate it was enough." Her arms link around my neck. "It was supposed to be a quiet, understated rebellion."

"And then you woke up with a hangover from hell."

"And you fast-talked me into coming with you anyway." Her fingers sift into my hair. "Thank you, Wade."

With Harlow in my arms like this, peering up at me with those big soulful sweet eyes, I'm the one who's thankful. But not to her douche father, even if he's the reason she said yes.

"I gotta ask. What are you doing working for him? You're so damn smart, driven. You could do anything you wanted. Anywhere."

The way she deflates in my arms makes me wish I could take it back, but I don't get it. Anyone else would want her. Value her.

"I guess I keep hoping that one of these days I'll have the chance to prove myself. And maybe if he can see what I'm capable of, he'll realize he's been missing out. I know it doesn't seem like much, but he and Junior, as much of a troll as he is, are the only family I have. My mother's parents were dead before she left for school. There aren't any relatives." She takes a shaky breath. "The closest thing to a family I have is the bank. I've put everything I am into it… and I'm not ready to walk away."

Harlow

WE SPEND the next two days running errands for the wedding, hopping from house to house and helping out wherever we can. I've made cookies with Grace and filled mesh bags of birdseed with Janie's sisters while Wade worked with Walt and the guys, getting the space at the farm ready for the wedding and reception.

And around the myriad pre-wedding tasks, Wade keeps finding ways to get me alone. To pull me into his arms and tease me into the kind of breathless laughter I've never known.

It feels so good to be with him. So good to be a part of something. So good, that every time I think about what's on the other side of Sunday... I just can't.

I don't want to waste a minute thinking about anything but how right everything feels now.

Hearing the thud of Wade's truck in the drive, my heart skips and a hundred butterflies erupt into flight in my belly.

Grace pats my hand at her kitchen table where she's been showing me the album from her wedding. "Go say hi, honey. I'm going to put these away."

I'm out of my seat in a too-eager, too-obvious blink. "Be right back."

She chuckles, waving me away. "Sure you will."

Heat fills my cheeks as I push through the front door, this insane sense of urgency in my chest that's begging me to move faster, get closer.

Wade's halfway to the house. He looks up, our eyes meet, and he drops his bags as I fling myself into his arms. Laugh at the utter relief of having my body flush against his, the dizzying joy of him spinning me around, and the light in his eyes as he carries me back to the truck—to the far side of the truck—and kisses the life out of me. Gives me his tongue in slow, measured thrusts. Bunches my hair in his fists, pulling just enough to remind me of the night before.

The screen door closes at the house. "Don't mind me," comes Grace's singsong voice, full of amusement. "Gonna bring this ice cream inside real quick."

Wade presses a last kiss to my lips, then calls over the roof of the car, "Thanks, Mom. Be right there."

My fingers run over the planes of his face, down the thick column of his neck, stilling over his chest. "One more minute," I whisper.

Those blue eyes search mine. "Long as you want, Good Girl."

We stay for dinner with the Gradys. Walt is flying solo tonight as Janie is having a final fitting and then dinner with her family. We're out on the back patio, done eating, the bottle of wine Wade brought empty, but no one is in a rush to get up.

It's quiet and comfortable. And even with Kelsey ignoring me from across the table, it's the sort of evening a girl could get used to.

Grace smiles between her son and me. "We've been so caught up in the plans for Janie and Walt this week, I just realized I haven't heard how the two of you met."

Bill leans over the table, a wide smile on his face. "Come on, let's hear it. I'm thinking this guy threw some smooth line your way and had a date on the books before you knew what hit you."

It's pretty adorable the way this man thinks his sons can do no wrong. Or who knows, maybe they can't, and what I really love is that he sees it.

Walt snorts, the imp in his eyes firing up. "Yeah, did he take you out to the malt shop and steal a lick off your sundae?"

I choke a bit on my water, laughing at how dirty these Grady boys are. But then an uneasy feeling settles in the pit of my stomach. Grace wants to know how we met and I don't want to lie to Wade's family anymore. But telling the truth isn't an option.

I open my mouth, ready to stick with the story, when Wade cuts in. "Ha, I wish. Hate to let you down, but Harlow doesn't actually remember the first time we met."

Brows go up around the table and, caught off guard, I turn to my date and gape. "What? I remember." Sure, the details were a little… blurry.

Wade presses a finger to my mouth and his mom claps. Everyone leans forward except Kelsey, who sits stone still.

With the room's attention, he starts again. "I'd been over at the bank for an appointment and after, I'm taking the elevator down. On one of the floors, this gorgeous girl steps in beside me, pretty nose buried so far in some report, she doesn't even notice when I throw not one, not two, but *three* solid lines her way."

I'm not breathing. There's no way it's true. I don't know why he'd make it up, unless he wants to give us a more romantic story than the one we have.

"Totally shuts me down."

At which point Walt rocks back in his chair, fists pumping air. "Yes! Harlow, you are my favorite."

"Did you not hear him?" Kelsey snaps, and Grace gives her a worried glance.

Wade doesn't stop. "So I tap her arm and ask what time it is, thinking she'll look up. Our eyes will meet. She'll fall under the spell of my smile and charm, and I'll be *eating her sundae* before the night's through."

"Wade!" I laugh.

"She checks her watch, like on her actual wrist." He holds up my arm to show off the slender band. "Mutters the time to me and then breaks a speed-walking record leaving the elevator."

I turn to him. "I had no idea."

His eyes are gleaming. "My ego begged me not to recount his brush with death."

"I should have looked," I say quietly.

"Ehh, the timing wasn't right. But it all worked out." Then back to the table, "A few months later she shows up in this club where I'm hanging out with Boomer, Axe, and Bowie. FYI, she still wasn't into me. Was sure her dad wouldn't like me."

Grace clucks her tongue. "Everyone likes you, honey."

But Walt raises a brow. "This why there isn't a single picture of you two on social?"

Wade shrugs, not exactly confirming or denying before he goes on. "Didn't think jocks were her type."

And whoa, talk about a bombshell.

His parents gasp, for real, which makes me laugh even harder as I hold up my hands. "I swear, I've since reconsidered!"

Kelsey straightens, her smile stiff. "You're not into sports?" She shakes her head. "How is that going to work? Wade's whole life is about sports. He's a *professional* athlete. And when he's done in the NHL, he's moving back here to coach our Tigers hockey team."

I turn to Wade, surprised. "Really, you want to coach like your dad?"

But he's sort of wagging his head noncommittally. "I don't know. I used to think so, but who knows." He smiles at me. "It's a long ways off and a lot can change."

Kelsey looks like she's about to have an aneurysm, but I'm still thinking about Wade as a coach. He'd be amazing with kids.

Taking my hand, he brings it up to his mouth for a kiss. Rubs his thumb over the knuckles in a soft stroke. "Back to my story. I needed a date for some event and finally talked her into it. And FYI, I'm totally her type. It just took some convincing."

My heart melts. Because Wade just gave his parents the truth of how our relationship began so I wouldn't have to lie to his family.

Chapter 21

Wade

I don't know what it is, but something's changed between us. I saw it in Harlow's smile when I got back to the house today. Felt it in the clutch of her hands on my chest when she wanted that minute more.

And tonight, it's in the kiss she gives me when we get to the truck. It's slow and sweet. Lingering. And when her eyes come up and meet mine—yeah, something's changed.

We don't spill into the hotel room, tearing at each other's clothes like we can't waste a second of the precious time we've got left. We walk in together, fingers tangled in a loose hold. I sit in the wingback chair by the window and pull Harlow onto my lap.

"I didn't know about the elevator," she says, playing with my knuckles.

"It was epic."

"It's sad." She shakes her head. "Wade, you were right there, and I missed you. I didn't even notice. Why? Because of some regulatory report? Because I was killing myself for a job I didn't even get?"

"Harlow," I start, but when her eyes come up to meet mine, they're brimming with tears. They gut me, have my heart beating harder as I hold her close. "Don't cry."

"I don't want to miss any more."

I slip a hand around her neck and draw her in for a kiss. Then, holding her in my arms, I cross to the bed where we lie down together. Fully dressed, shoes off.

"Okay, Good Girl. No more missing out." She nestles closer, peering up at me from my shoulder. "Tell me. What's the first thing we're going to do when we get back to Chicago?"

Jesus, those eyes. That look.

I know what I want it to mean. I know how I feel.

It's too soon. But there's no rush.

Finding my voice, I tease, "But keep it on this side of the law. I like to keep my nose clean."

Wade

IT'S STILL DARK. Harlow's legs are entwined with mine, her body tucked close.

We're both early risers, but this seems—

I hear it then. The repetitive vibration of her phone from where it's charging beside the bed.

"Good Girl," I murmur, hating to wake her, but I know she's got her phone on Do Not Disturb, which means whoever is calling at 4:37 a.m. must be important. "Your phone's ringing."

She lifts her head, sleepy and adorable. Confused.

"Harlow. Your phone."

Her eyes clear, and she fumbles for the phone, almost knocking a lamp over in the process. But then she's got it. I can't see the screen, but the voice booming through the line can only be one man.

And I hate him.

"Harlow, Junior totaled his car."

"Is—is he okay?" She staggers from the bed, her voice stricken.

I slip out the other side, flipping the light on and coming around to rest my hand at her back.

I'm already making plans in my head. I'll pack while she gets the details. Drive her back today. Be back for the wedding tomorrow, depending—

"He's in the hospital." Irritation snaps through the

line. "Says the drugs were the girl's. Escort. Press got to her before we could and—" He sighs. "Going to be a damn mess to clean up this time."

Harlow stares at the phone like she doesn't know what to say. And yeah, it's a lot to unpack. "He's in the hospital? God, how bad was he hurt? Does… Sandy know?"

There's a beat of cold silence and she physically winces from it. I'm about to take that fucking phone myself when he answers. "Sprained wrist. Some bruises. He's my son. He'll be fine. But I've decided he'll go to rehab."

Her breath comes out in a rush, and she nods. They aren't close, but this is the only family she has.

"I'm glad it wasn't more serious. But maybe rehab will be a good thing for him."

"It's the best place to park him until this blows over."

Harlow's eyes cut to mine and she mouths an apology. I shake my head and hold her hand. Then, giving her the most reassuring smile I've got, I mouth the word "coffee" and point at the door.

Gratitude fills her eyes and she sits down at the desk, picking up the pen and notepad. "What can I do?"

I stuff my legs into my jeans and pull on a shirt. Grab my wallet.

A throat clears from across the miles. "Obviously, this changes things. In the short term, we'll have to distance Junior from PHR. Be at the office at eight."

"What?" she chokes out, and I stop halfway out the door.

But instead of turning to me, she turns farther away, her shoulders hunching forward.

Privacy. Damn it, I don't want to leave. If she'd turned toward me, I'd be back at her side. But that's not what she needs right now. So I close the door behind me. The last thing I hear is her asshole father saying the words Harlow's been waiting her whole life to hear.

"You want to prove yourself? Here's your chance."

I make it to the truck before giving in to the string of expletives clawing at my throat.

This thing between us is too new to compete with the approval of the douchebag who's been neglecting her, her whole life. We've barely begun and I'm going to lose her.

I drive to the gas station and fill up the truck. Clean the windows and check the tires, telling myself not to be a dick by trying to talk her out of going back. Not to remind her of all the shabby shit her father has put her through, when for what sounds like the first time in her life, he's giving her the credit she deserves.

Only an asshole would try to take that away from her, and that's not who I want to be to her. Harlow needs a fucking good guy, even if that means I need to drive her back to Chicago and say goodbye in front of the PHR corporate headquarters, knowing there's a damn good chance there won't be a place for me in her life after that.

The life she'd been so desperate to escape for a week. Ten days.

Fuck.

I spend the drive to the coffee shop telling myself it's not over. That come Monday, she'll want to continue from where we're leaving off. That I'll pick her up from work and she'll throw her arms around my neck, telling me she missed me even though it's only been a couple days. That it doesn't matter that her petty, piece-of-shit father won't approve of me based on my career choice alone. That even though Harlow has spent her entire life killing herself to impress this guy, she'll still choose to give us a chance. Because she feels it too. Because this thing between us is different… it's real.

And then I spend the ride back to the hotel telling myself to get my shit together and act like a fucking man because chances are good none of that is going to happen. Harlow is getting a shot at the one thing she's always wanted, and I'm not going to get in her way.

No matter how hard it will be.

I get up to the room and, bracing with a supportive

face that's backed with a steely will usually reserved for going *after* what I want rather than letting it go, let myself in. Stop short, not understanding what I'm seeing.

"Where's the coffee?" Harlow asks from within the still tangled sheets of our bed. Her hair is still a sexy sleep-mussed mess. She's still swimming in my T-shirt, our clothes from the night before still scattered around the room.

There aren't any bags. Just the woman I could feel slipping through my fingers, looking like she isn't going anywhere.

I rub my hand over the spot in my chest that's hammering harder than it did before my first NHL game.

"In the truck. With breakfast." Water. Soda. Some snacks and, in case she wanted to try and sleep on the way back, one of those neck pillow things that people love but would straight-up strangle me. "You're not packed."

I don't want to jump to conclusions. Hell, she might only want to sleep another hour or so. She might—

Jesus, *please* be what it looks like.

Harlow

"I'M NOT LEAVING," I say quietly, somehow more nervous than I was on the phone with my father. Wade doesn't move and the anxiety that's been building since he left ramps higher. What if he doesn't want—

But then, he's on me in a blink, pulling me hard against him, crushing me with his kiss. Telling me everything I need to know without words.

I cling to him, emotion choking me.

"Thought I was losing you," he growls against my mouth, arms banded around my back, holding me so my bare feet dangle above the floor.

"No."

Not when it feels like, for the first time in my life, I'm not missing what matters. I'm not *alone*.

"I was going to take you." He lays me back on the bed, following me down. "Let you go if that's what you needed." He whips the shirt off my body and does the same with his clothes. Groans when we're skin to skin. Then pulls back to meet my eyes. "Fuck, Harlow, it was going to kill me."

I shake my head, run my fingers over his scruff. "I told him I couldn't leave and I'd be there Monday." And then the truth I need him to know. "I couldn't leave you."

"Just for this week?"

"What if it's more than this week?" I ask softly.

His eyes close and then he kisses me again, so long

and deep, when he stops, we're tangled together. "So you're mine, really mine?"

Mine.

No one has ever wanted me to be theirs. And the way this man does, so openly, so completely… it makes my heart ache so hard I can barely breathe through it.

Hands shaking, I trace the lines of his face. Slip my knee higher up his ribs. Inviting. "I'm yours."

God, the sound he makes. It's pure possessive relief.

And then he's pushing inside me. Thick and long. Slow and gentle.

He fills my body the way he's filling my heart. Completely. And when it feels like he's given me all I can take, he says my name with quiet reverence… and gives me that much more.

We move together. Eyes locked. Bodies straining.

It's beautiful.

It's making love. My first time. And I never want to stop.

Chapter 22

Wade

She's mine.

Knowing it—hearing her say it once should have been enough. But I'm like a damn addict, needing more, again, louder. Coaxing, teasing, and working it out of her... On my knees with her hands in my hair, her back against the door to our room, the taste of her coating my tongue. Her breathless cries falling like soft rain over my shoulders.

Against the shower wall, while I give her my cock so slow and good. She says it *twice*.

On. The. Pull-out.

I give her everything I have. *Almost* everything.

I want to tell her how hot and sweet she is. I want her to hear how she makes me feel. That nothing has ever been so good. But I don't dare say a damn word, because if I open my mouth when we're that close, when I can feel her heart beating against mine... I'm going to tell her something it's too soon to say.

Something that when she hears it the first time, I want her to believe with her whole heart and never doubt.

Eventually, we make it out to the truck and the abandoned travel smorgasbord.

"You really went all out," she says with the kind of soft, satisfied smile I'd like to keep on her lips for the next fifty years or so.

But when she tries to reach for the hours-cold coffee in her drink holder, I swat her hand away. "No. This one's no good." Fucking tainted with heartbreak, and she's not getting one sip.

I collect every single thing I bought before dawn including the neck pillow. I even take the charger I'd plugged in for her phone, and I dump the entire lot of it into the trash bin by the lobby door.

When I get back, Harlow's staring at me like I'm out of my mind. But I just slide into my seat, take her hand in mine, and lean over to kiss her. Quick. Because the sun's up and my gorgeous Good Girl was already embarrassed by the noise we made earlier.

I should feel guilty, but *fuuuck*, once I found that spot that made her scream... no way was I giving that up.

"You get *fresh* coffee and a *hot* breakfast."

She's still playing with my knuckles. Damn, that's nice. "When are we supposed to be at your mom's?"

Half an hour ago, but I already texted that we were running late. "After I get you fed."

Harlow

I KEEP WAITING for the nerves. The uncertainty. The looming sense of dread that always accompanies the slightest hint of resistance to my father's dictates. But it doesn't come. Not at eight, when I was supposed to be at work. Not through breakfast. Not once Wade parks me in his high school bedroom and tells me to get some sleep while he and his parents run a few last errands.

It's like, for the very first time, every single part of me is in agreement on what it wants. Like I know what matters most… and I'm not worried about losing it.

Wade's bed is comfortable and soft, the blue plaid comforter smells like fresh laundry. I barely remember lying down, but when I open my eyes, the light in the room is different and there's a weight at the foot of the bed.

For a heartbeat, I think it's Wade. But no.

I sit up fast. "Kelsey, what are you doing in here?"

She's sitting with her knees tucked neatly together, eyes rimmed in red, and a tragic smile on her face.

"When you first got here, I didn't know what to think. Wade never brings girls home. And I didn't really see—" She takes a breath and holds up her hands with a helpless laugh. "I thought, she's all wrong. It can't last. I even let myself think maybe you weren't really together. But I see it now."

Her being in here while I'm sleeping is beyond inappropriate, and it isn't even close to the oversteps she's taken with Wade. But more than ever, I can understand why Kelsey hasn't been able to get over Wade. If I lost him, I'm not sure I could.

I wouldn't be like this, but I feel for her.

"I care about him very much." I love him. It took me by surprise, but there it is. And while I'm sure, the first time I say those words, it will be to him.

A nod, and she pushes up from the bed. Walks to the bookcase filled with trophies and medals. "He deserves someone who will love him. Through thick and thin. I thought it could be me." A fresh tear slips free. "But he wants it to be you."

"I'm sorry, Kelsey." What else is there to say?

"Me too." And then with a last sad smile, she leaves the room.

I take a minute to absorb what just happened. I hear the front door close and then the sound of an engine turning over. The house is quiet and when I make my way downstairs, there's a note on the kitchen table.

Kelsey's getting ready at a friend's.

When I text Wade, he calls me back within seconds.

"She was sitting on the bed?"

He sounds pissed.

"It was weird, definitely. But, Wade… I think your fake girlfriend plan actually worked."

"*Real* girlfriend. You agreed. You're mine." His voice drops to a seductive whisper that stirs another needy ache low in my center. How is that even possible? "But I'm happy to leave my parents with the chair rental truck and come back there to remind you, Good Girl."

"Don't abandon your parents, please. I want them to like me. But feel free to remind me again once you're back."

He growls through the line and I practically float into the living room.

"Wade, I'm serious, though. Maybe this was exactly what you were hoping with Kelsey. Maybe she needed to see you with someone else."

"Maybe she needed to see me with *you*."

My heart warms. "Maybe you should hurry back here. See if we can sneak off for an hour before the rehearsal."

There's some rustling from his end, like he might be covering the phone. Then a muffled, "Dad, let's wrap it up... tell Mom I'll buy her both." Then more clearly, "On my way."

TURNS out the hour we were hoping for ends up being more like ten minutes. But they're ten minutes I put to good use getting Wade to tell *me* emphatically, repeatedly, and interspersed with a string of unintelligible cursing, that he's *mine*.

Who knew a girl could get such a power trip being on her knees?

We make it to the farm for the rehearsal with a few minutes to spare. Janie's family is fussing over her and Walt in their matching *Bride* and *Groom* T-shirts. There are cousins on ladders stringing LED lanterns around the grove that borders the clearing where the tables will be set up. And the Gradys are all smiles and hugs as we walk over to where some relation on one side or the other is coordinating the dry run.

I step off to the side where a smattering of dates hang back, watching as the bridesmaids and groomsmen are paired up and given instructions.

There's a tiny blond girl with bright blue eyes running around like an adorable terror. And when

Wade catches her on her next pass, parking her in the crook of his arm… well, that is some potent stuff.

I don't notice that Janie's come up beside me until she pulls me away from the group.

"Janie, this place is amazing," I say, meaning it completely.

She nods, looking around. But when her eyes cut back to mine, there's apology in them. "Harlow, when we started planning this, I had no idea Wade was dating someone." I find Wade across the clearing and immediately know what she's referring to.

He's standing a polite distance away from Kelsey, but they are definitely paired up.

Janie bites her lip. "If I'd had any idea how she would behave when he brought someone home, I would never have—"

"Janie, *no*. Seriously, don't give it a second thought. Kelsey and I are *fine*." Mostly. Fine enough, anyway. "It's all good. Promise. Now get up there."

She gives my hand a squeeze. "Pay attention. This could be you guys in not too long."

The rehearsal goes off without a hiccup, and the dinner after is at a local barbecue place where Janie and Walt had their first date. I catch Bill wiping a tear from the corner of his eye when Walt stands up and gives a speech about why he's so lucky to be marrying Janie. Grace beams and Wade squeezes my hand, giving me a look that makes me believe anything is possible.

Back at the hotel, I sleep in Wade's arms and wake up to him peppering kisses across my body.

Saturday is a day of smiles and joyful tears, dancing, and laughter. A day that ends with Wade loving me right on into the next morning and me wondering how this can be my life.

And then our ten days is over.

Chapter 23

Wade

*H*arlow spends most of the ride back to Chicago handling email from her phone. We have lunch at a dive known for their cinnamon rolls and hold hands across the table, talking about the wedding. We stop at the gas station where we had our first practice run at the *physical stuff* and end up making out in the truck until someone honks and we remember where we are.

It's pretty excellent.

But nothing beats that moment when we cross into city limits and Harlow asks me if I'll stay the night with her. Hell, yes, I will.

I stay that night and the next, and the next after that, Nettie comes over with a bottle of wine and a sleeve of Pringles, which she devours as Harlow gives her the highlights reel of our trip and fake-to-really-real relationship. Or the PG version anyway.

She's back at work, happy to be doing the job that should have been hers from the start. I ask about her dad, but she hasn't actually seen him since she's been back.

My guess, he's being a prick because she didn't drop everything to come running the second he called.

Probably a good thing we're planning to give it some time before I meet him.

For now, my off-season life is getting back to normal.

Harlow left for work an hour ago and I'm getting an early workout in with the guys. "Grady, put a few pounds on the bar. Christ, Piper could lift more than that." Piper is Boomer's little sister, and he's talking shit because I lift a fuck-ton more than he can. Not that that's ever stopped the guy. "The sport drink guys are gonna yank your endorsement with those girlie arms."

"Uh-huh." The sport drink guys flew in to meet with me yesterday and asked how few clothes I'd be willing to wear in their ads. I think I'm okay.

The only thing giving me hives is my Slayers contract. My agent, Pete Greer, says not to sweat it. They're offering, it's just a matter of the details. The guy's been at this a long time, so I believe him, but still.

I'll feel a hell of a lot better when the ink is dry and I'm celebrating with Harlow over a bottle of bubbly.

I move in beside Bowie for squats, and we're talking about how strange it's going to be to play next season without Popov and whether anyone's heard anything more about Baxter when my phone pings with an alert. And then another and another. The guys set their weights down, same as me. My gut goes off because there shouldn't be anything to report until I sign.

Then it comes. Pete's ringtone, and I sweep up my phone, heart pounding. This is what I've been waiting for. What I've been working for.

"Hey, man, my phone's blowing up. What's going on?"

Before he answers, the guys' phones start to ping and vibrate too.

Axe mutters a weighted curse and holds up his phone to show me.

And my world comes crashing down around me.

"Oh *fuck*." I need to find Harlow. Now.

Harlow

THE WORKDAY HAS BARELY BEGUN, and I've already got two people in my office with two more waiting outside the door.

I don't know what Junior spent his time on before his accident, but it wasn't this job. He ordered business cards and stationery—there's a ton of it. And pens. Fountain pens from Mont Blanc. But the flagged wire transfers that have been moving up the line stopped with him, along with pretty much every other request that's come through in the past two weeks.

I found a pad with some notes I can barely read, not that it would have mattered since, after about three lines, he started sketching a woman in a bikini with her breasts spilling out of her scanty top.

This is the guy my father chose over me. I'm trying to be sympathetic, but it's a challenge. Junior's in rehab in Aspen. I called to check on him Sunday, but he had a massage scheduled so he couldn't talk to me directly. But from what Amber relayed during the brief call, he was bored but fine. And he wanted me to know that I could keep my job because it "sucked."

Carrie and Tim are still working down their lists when there's a hard rap on my door and my father's assistant ducks in.

"Dan, what can I do for you?"

His cheeks are red, thinning hair spiked like he's

sweating. "Harlow, I'm sorry to interrupt, but Philip needs you in his office."

I blink. "Sure, of course. Let me wrap things up here and—"

He gives a sharp shake of his head. "He said *now*."

And now Dan's not the only one with a red face. I excuse myself, trying to ignore the too-polite smiles and then the wide-eyed exchanges between coworkers as I follow, then follow faster through the corridors.

When I get to Philip's office, I smooth my hands over my suit and hair. But taking a second to compose myself takes too long, and my father's voice snaps from beyond his door.

"*Now*, Harlow."

I have no idea what's happening. Dan won't even look at me.

"Philip, what's going on?" I ask with a calm I'm not feeling.

He's parked behind an enormous desk, black suit immaculate, not a hair out of place. Eyes an arctic blue so cold they chill me to the bone. His voice is even colder. "I give you a chance and this is how you repay me?"

I can barely breathe. My hands come up in question. "I'm sorry. I don't know—"

"You should be. If you don't have enough respect

for yourself, I at least expect you to have it for PHR. For me."

He shakes his head in disgust, tossing a sheaf of papers across the high-polish mahogany. The first thing I see is a picture from the wedding. It's Wade and I standing together, his front to my back, his arms around me. Our heads tipped together.

It's beautiful.

"Philip," I whisper. "He's a good man. The best. He's—"

But then I see it. The next picture isn't as clear, it's older. But even without his name in bold letters, there would be no mistaking that the man—*the boy*—in the mugshot is Wade Grady.

"Another junkie. Worse. That's an arrest for *intent to sell*."

"No. He doesn't do drugs. Dad—Philip," I correct at his indignant cough, "where did you get this?" Based on the date, Wade would have been a minor. This should be sealed.

That night at the bar comes back to me. That bad blood with Collin, the guy who'd been the fuckup that nearly cost Wade his future. This has to be what he was talking about. "Let me call him. There's an explanation. I know there is. This isn't who Wade is. He's so careful. He's—"

God, he's *waiting on a contract*.

Examining the printouts, I can see they came off the web. It's from one of the hockey sites I'd been skimming before the wedding.

This picture is already out.

"We'll sort this out. But I need to call Wade." He must be going out of his mind.

"What you need to do is lose this player's number. End it. Now."

I didn't hear him right. I couldn't have. "Excuse me?"

"I won't be embarrassed by you any more than I already have."

"Dad—"

"Harlow. Remember where you are."

I look around, and it's like I'm seeing it for the first time.

"I know exactly where I am. I'm in my father's office. Having a disagreement about the man I love."

His laugh is like a slap in the face. "This isn't about love. It's not even about whether there's some explanation, as you say. It's about perception. It's about showing you're capable of putting this bank, this family, first. We don't need this kind of association tainting our image." He meets me with his level stare. "You've been desperate for my attention your whole life. Congratulations. You've got it. Think twice before you throw it away for some *jock*."

Wade

MOTHERFUCKER!

I can't reach her. I've called her phone a hundred times. Got in a cab and started heading to her office. Called the bank, lost my fucking mind getting passed from department to department, put on hold so long that I was actually in the lower atrium of PHR headquarters when I finally got Nettie on the line. But she didn't know much more than I did. Harlow was apparently gone for the day and she wasn't answering her phone.

This is bad.

Her name was listed with mine in the picture from the wedding. Her father's and the bank too. This is everything she didn't want, everything she was afraid of.

No.

This is one hundred times worse.

I should have told her about the arrest. When she asked about Collin, I should have explained in detail, right fucking then.

But hell, there was just so much going on.

I wasn't hiding it. I figured I'd tell her someday, but it never even occurred to me that she'd find out about it like this. The charges had been dismissed. The records sealed. Hell, I'd actually thought the courthouse had them incinerated at some point.

So I didn't tell her that at fifteen, he'd hidden drugs in my truck without me knowing it, then let me get *arrested* before coming clean. That he'd been the close call that could have cost me my career before I even had it. And now that close call has the potential to cost me Harlow.

Now I'm pacing in front of her apartment—Pete bellowing in my ear—praying she'll come home, and when she does, she'll give me the chance to explain.

"This is your career, Grady! Get your ass down here now."

I shove a hand through my hair. He doesn't get it. *This is my life.*

And then I see her coming around the corner and my heart stops. "I'll call you back."

I run down the block, my gut in knots.

Jesus, the hair that had been pinned into a perfect twist when I kissed her goodbye this morning hangs around her shoulders. Her eyes are red… and she's fighting to get what looks like a phone out of some plastic clamshell.

"Harlow," I pant, stopping in front of her. Ready to drop to my knees and beg her to believe that what's been circulating isn't the truth. To give me the chance to explain.

Her eyes meet mine and she drops everything and throws her arms around me. "Are you okay?" she gasps, clinging to me. "They took my phone and I—I didn't remember your number to call."

I pull her back, a new panic surging through me. "Who took your phone?"

Was she mugged? I'm checking her hands, her arms, her face—

"It was a company phone and when I left... Wade, your contract?"

My contract? That's what she's worried about?

"Harlow, why did you leave?"

Tears spill over her lids. "I quit. And thirty seconds later my father had security take my phone and walk me out. What happened—" She shakes her head and waves her hands around. "Wade, what happened today?"

"It's a mistake. A misunderstanding. Damn it, honestly, I have no idea what happened or how this thing got out. But the arrest was a mistake. That thing with Collin from high school I should have told you about. The drugs were his and they threw out the charges when he came forward. I'll explain, I-I will, but... You quit? Because of this?" The idea that I might have cost her the career she loves, something she's worked so hard for, makes me sick. She told me her father wouldn't approve. We talked about waiting to meet him. Letting her settle into her job first. Having a chance to prove herself. Christ.

And then her tyrant father finds out about her relationship from the news, and his first introduction to the guy she's dating is a damn mugshot.

This is all my fault.

"Wade, I quit because I finally had to accept some hard truths about my father and the impact I've been allowing—no, inviting him to have on my life."

"Harlow. I'm so sorry."

Her hand comes up to my face. "I'm not. The things he said to me today… I always thought he didn't see me. That he didn't realize who he had right there in front of his face. But he did. He knew exactly how hard I'd been trying to get his attention… and he just didn't want to give it to me." She sniffs, sucking a quick breath. "I finally realized his attention isn't worth having."

"But the bank." I know how she felt about that place.

Another shake of her head. "Before I met you, it felt like the bank was my whole life. I was afraid to lose it, but I don't think it was because I loved it. It was *all I had*. It was the one thing that connected me to my father, and without it… I thought I would have had nothing."

Christ, it kills me to think about how alone she's been and for how long.

"The thing is, I'm the reason my world was so small. I was so focused on this singular unattainable goal, I shut out everything else, telling myself I didn't have time, I didn't have room, I didn't need a life. And then I met you. And you showed me what I was missing. And I want it. I want a *life*. I want *love*. And most of all, I want *you*."

I brush a bit of hair from her face, tucking it behind her ear. "You have me. Harlow, I love you."

She blinks as more tears fill her eyes, only this time her beautiful smile accompanies them. "I love you too."

"Let's go inside. We can talk and—"

"Someone's seriously blowing up your phone."

She's right. It hasn't stopped going off since I hung up on Pete. "My agent. He wants me to come in, try to get ahead of this thing. But I—I need to know you're okay. *We're* okay."

Her brows shoot up and she wipes at her cheeks with the back of her wrist. "Wade, is this about your contract?"

And the endorsement. "Probably. Yes."

"*Wade!* Get on your phone and order a Lyft. You need to get over there."

Harlow

WADE DOESN'T WANT to leave me, so I go along to the meeting. They set me up in a comfortable conference room that feels more like a living room with its pro-athlete-sized leather couch and enormous coffee table. I set up the prepaid phone I bought at 7-Eleven with a list of numbers Wade wrote down for me. It's not a forever phone, but it's enough for me to call Grace.

She answers on the first ring. "I've been calling and calling. What's happening?"

"He's okay. He's been in meetings with his agent and they've got the lawyers involved. But mostly they're working on damage control with the Slayers."

I can hear Bill shouting at someone in the background, issuing threats I wouldn't want to be on the receiving end of.

And then from closer, Kelsey. "Is it Wade? Tell him I can come to Chicago and help. Stay as long as he needs. Anything."

I try not to bristle. We have bigger problems. So I ask, "Grace, I don't know how long it will be before Wade can talk, but does anyone have an idea how this got out?"

So far, the answer is no. But the Gradys' family and friends are making calls, checking to see if anyone's seen or heard anything.

Within an hour, the lawyers are getting results from their end. The news and gossip sites begin updating their stories, posting apologies, and removing the mugshot that never should have been taken, let alone released.

Wade comes to check on me between meetings and calls.

He's exhausted, but it's me he keeps worrying about, pulling me onto his lap and holding me quietly before going back for more. It pays off, and the Slayers contract comes through. Pete thinks the endorsement will too, but eventually he sends us home for the night.

It's not the celebration we'd planned, but it's been such a trying day and there's still so much up in the air, we order DoorDash and eat dinner on the couch and then crawl into bed together.

The next morning, Tommy's talked to Collin and swears the guy had nothing to do with the arrest getting out. It's a period of his life he's tried to put behind him, and even Wade doesn't think he's got anything to do with it.

But there's something in his eyes that has me sitting down beside him and taking his big hand in mine. "Wade. What's going on? Did you hear back from Pete?"

He shakes his head and holds up his phone for me to see.

Kelsey: Can we talk?

The hair on the back of my neck stands up. "You don't think…"

Scrubbing a hand over his face, he hits Call.

"She's still there?" comes Kelsey's flat voice through the line.

"Yes." Wade's head drops forward.

She sighs, and the answer no one wanted to consider is there in that hopeless sound. It was her. "I thought she would leave when she saw it. I thought she'd leave and you'd see that she wasn't the one for you. And then when the truth came out, you'd already know that she wasn't the woman who would stick by your side and love you through everything."

"Fuck, Kelsey. How could you do it? Why?"

"Because I've been here this whole time," she sniffs. "Right here, waiting for you to realize what you could have if you would *just take it*. Waiting for you to come home and have the life we're supposed to. You coaching hockey. Me, cheering you on."

Wade's eyes meet mine. We're both seeing it. The dinner with his family. Her shock that he might not come back to Enderson after the NHL. I text his parents. She loves them, and until today I'd have bet my life she would never hurt anyone in their family. But now I don't know.

She lets out a short laugh. "Instead, you choose

someone who doesn't understand you. Who would rather hide you from her family than stand proud beside you. I thought... maybe it was time for *you* to have a lesson in disappointment."

Grace's text comes back in seconds. Kelsey's not at the house. Her car is gone. Bill's calling the police.

"Where are you?" Wade asks, eyes bleak.

"The courthouse. I sent the files from work. I didn't think about it when I did it. But I heard Bill asking about tracing the emails... They're going to go back to my terminal."

"Jesus."

It's quiet for a moment, then she has to go. Her boss is there, and she's going to tell him what she's done.

When we update Pete and the lawyers, they think she's looking at fines more than jail time. She'll lose her job.

But Wade and I both know, the price that will be the hardest for her to pay will be losing his family.

I ask if Wade wants a minute to talk to his parents alone, but he pulls me into his side, holding me close as we call. Grace is a mess and Bill is quiet. They blame themselves, but Wade assures them it's not their fault. That he was the one who hadn't been honest enough about the situation with Kelsey.

And when I take his hand and quietly tell him I'm

sure… he explains the rest. About us. How it started. Where we are now. That he loves me.

And when Grace says she loves me too, I start crying again.

Wade

IT'S BEEN a fucked-up couple of days. But Harlow and I held each other through them and we're coming out the other side stronger. Together.

And now we're figuring out what life is going to look like going forward.

Spoiler: It's looking good.

Harlow's phone is the one blowing up these days. She's gotten a ton of offers already, and the headhunters keep coming. But she's taking her time and weighing her choices. Letting the PHR competition wine and dine her.

She's kind of delighted by the whole thing and, man, nothing's better than seeing that smile.

Pete was able to hang on to the endorsement. And to celebrate, we decided to move in together. Harlow's the one who brought it up, but I'd been thinking about it since the night we got back from Enderson. So it didn't take much dirty talking to get me on board.

The guys are giving me relentless shit. Not about Harlow—they love her. But about the whole "be the bunny" business. So needless to say, Axel has been running his mouth. I can't wait for the day he meets the right girl and I get to pay him back with interest.

Hell, what am I thinking? This guy's a contender for the Lifetime Player Award. He'll never settle down.

Besides, "Be the bunny" got me Harlow.

So life is good. I love Harlow. My family loves Harlow. And my friends love her too. Now I just need to get my girl to love hockey.

Epilogue

Harlow
One Month Later

"Grace, I can't believe you did this!" I'm parked on our living room sofa with Grace on speaker, the contents of the care package she sent spread out on the coffee table before me. Wade's working out and won't be home for a few hours, but this package was addressed to me and me alone. *And I couldn't wait!*

There's an assortment of flavored teas, a tiny vial of glitter that's sealed with a sticker that has Wade's name on it with a giant X through it. There's a tin of homemade cookies and a leather-bound book that made me cry when I opened it.

She started a scrapbook for us.

And Wade must have known, because there's a crazy bad picture that has to be from his phone, taken from the night at the club. There are receipts from all the gas stations we stopped at on the way to Enderson and then picture after picture—some I didn't even realize had been taken—of us with his family and us with his friends. Of us starting something real.

It took me several tissues to get past that one. But then she asked if I'd seen what else she sent. And sure enough, there was more.

"Cheat sheets?" I ask, laughing at the binder she compiled with the Slayers team roster and a short dossier on each of the players with the information she found most interesting about them.

Spoiler: It's not their stats. And Grace noticed the same thing about Boomer's little sister, Piper, and Bowie that I did.

"I know how you like to study up on everything. And seeing as how you're an official hockey girlfriend, I thought this might be a good way to start."

There's a list of hockey terminology. Websites for gossip and news. Pictures of Wade on every team he's played with—including football—with his numbers and stats. Team rivalries and traded players.

All in clear plastic page protectors that make me love this woman even more than I thought I could.

"Go to the back," she tells me, excitement in her voice.

I flip through and find several more pages with burned CDs tucked into sleeves and labeled with pictures of Wade dressed in his hockey gear.

"Are these his games?"

"In order. As many as we had from all the way back to Mites. He was so cute. I snuck a couple of his old football games in there too. He was spectacular."

When we hang up, I dig around to find something to play them on and then put the first one in.

I don't even know how many hours I've been sitting here, but I'm perched on the edge of the couch, my hands clutched in front of me, breath held, riveted to the last seconds of a game played six years ago. Wade's doing the impossible… on *skates*. He takes the puck off his opponent's stick. Passes it through the other guy's legs to *himself*.

And then he's blazing up the ice, feinting right and then cutting left, his stick a blur of motion. There's no time left. He fires off a shot and—

"*Score*," comes a low, familiar rumble at my ear, scaring the life and a totally humiliating yelp out me.

I'm off the couch in a flash, hand at my throat, eyes wide and shifting between the flesh-and-blood man in front of me and the miniature version of him pumping his fist hard as he glides on one skate into the embrace of a team that has spilled onto the ice following the final buzzer.

I'm mesmerized by both. In awe.

Wade grins down at the table. "Mom's package came."

He flips through the pages and shoots me a cocky, too-sexy grin. "Been watching my old games?"

Three of them. One from this past season with the Slayers, an AHL game, and this one from college. "You're really good."

Geez, was that breathy voice mine?

He straightens. His brows go high, and his mouth tips into that criminally hot, slanted smile.

"Good Girl—*oomf!*"

Wade catches me against him as I kiss him with the frantic need of a rabid fangirl, my legs locked at his back.

"So I'm guessing"—he takes my kiss—"the hockey"—gives me his—"works for you."

"So hot." My legs tighten, bringing us closer. "You're going to take me to your games?"

"Wrap you up in my number," he growls, hands moving to my ass to drag me over him.

"Number *seventeen*." I know it now. "Tap the glass when you skate by for warm-up."

"Hell, yes." We both groan. "Score for you."

"Wade." Heat spills through my center as he fills my

mouth with the thrust of his tongue, kissing me hard and deep. Backing me to the wall and grinding against that spot I need him most. "Tell me I'm yours."

"*Fuuuck*, Harlow. You're mine."

Yeah, I've got his number. But it works for me too.

"Make me *feel it*," I pant against his lips, reveling in his answering sound of masculine desperation. In the way he maneuvers me to pull down my leggings and panties on one side, so I can pull my leg free. In the way he bites his lip as he strokes through the spread of my sex.

I'm drenched for him. Quaking beneath his touch.

He gives me one thick finger, pumping in and out. "You feel that, Good Girl?"

"*Yes.*"

Another thick finger presses in with the first. Stroking. His touch making me whimper. "How about that?"

"So good."

"You want me to fuck you with my fingers?" He's at my ear, his teeth nipping at my lobe, tongue tracing the shell. "Give you another and fill you so good you come all over them?"

"Wade," I gasp, clenching around the stretch of a third. God, his hands are so big. His fingers so long. But I want— "More. *Please.*"

One more pump inside me and he eases out. The

emptiness is unbearable, but then he's back, the wide head of his cock nudging at me. Teasing. Torturing.

Making me crazy.

"You want me to make you feel it?"

I'm nodding, tipping my hips into his.

He drives in, full length. Filling me with everything I can take. More.

"Tell me," I whisper, trembling around him, my body already on the brink.

"You're mine." And then he starts to move, retreating only to take me deep again. Deeper. "Mine." Harder. "Been waiting for you forever." So good. "Never letting you go." So close. Almost *there*. "Fuck, I love you."

And then we're coming together, rocking, eyes locked, bodies as close as they can be.

My hands move to his face, my thumbs brushing across his short beard. "I love you too."

Thank you for reading DIRTY TALKER!! Want to see what Wade & Harlow are up to next? For a sweet and sexy **bonus epilogue**... **CLICK HERE to sign up for my newsletter!**

And Axel's story is next... **CLICK HERE to order DIRTY DEAL**

Also by Mira Lyn Kelly

SLAYERS HOCKEY

DIRTY SECRET (Vaughn & Natalie)

DIRTY HOOKUP (Quinn & George)

DIRTY REBOUND (Rux & Cammy)

DIRTY TALKER (Wade & Harlow)

BACK TO YOU

HARD CRUSH (Hank & Abby)

DIRTY PLAYER (Greg & Julia)

DIRTY BAD BOY (Jack & Laurel)

COMING AROUND AGAIN (McTark Re-releases)

Just Friends (Matt & Nikki)

All In (Lanie & Jason)

Acknowledgments

Fun fact: There's more to creating a book than just writing the words. A lot more!

The magic that goes into each book that finds it's way onto your eReader or shelf extends from that first willing ear to beyond the last set of eyes checking for typos. And I am beyond grateful for every single one of the people continually proving that writing is a team sport.

So huge thanks to Lexi Ryan, Lisa Kuhne, Jennifer Haymore, Kara Hildebrand, Sandra Shipman, Karin Enders, Crystal Perkins, Lori Rattay, Jessica Alcazar, Annika Martin, Zoe York, Skye Warren, Najla Qamber Designs, J. Ashley Photography, Tara Carberry, the team at Crazy Maple Studio, and Nicole Resciniti. To all the girls from Write All The Words, the PJ Party, my Promo team and Eagle Eyes, and the reviewers and bloggers who help me spread the word about my books. To my family who puts up with my crazy hours and pig pen office and my friends who are the best break from deadline crazy.

And especially to you! Thank you for reading.

((HUGS)) Mira

About the Author

Hard core romantic, stress baker, and housekeeper non-extraordinaire, Mira Lyn Kelly is the USA TODAY bestselling author of more than a dozen sizzly love stories with over a million readers worldwide. Growing up in the Chicago area, she earned her degree in Fine Arts from Loyola University and met the love of her life while studying abroad in Rome, Italy… only to discover he'd been living right around the corner from her back home. Having spent her twenties working and playing in the Windy City, she's now settled with her husband in Minnesota, where their four amazing children and two ridiculous dogs provide an excess of action and entertainment. www.miralynkelly.com

Looking to stay in touch and keep up with my new releases, sales and giveaways?? Join my newsletter at miralynkelly.com/newsletter and my Facebook reader group at MiraLynKellyPJParty. We'd love to have you!!

Made in the USA
Monee, IL
22 March 2021